MARVEL

MARVEL ACTION

SPIDER-MAN

SPIDER-CHASE

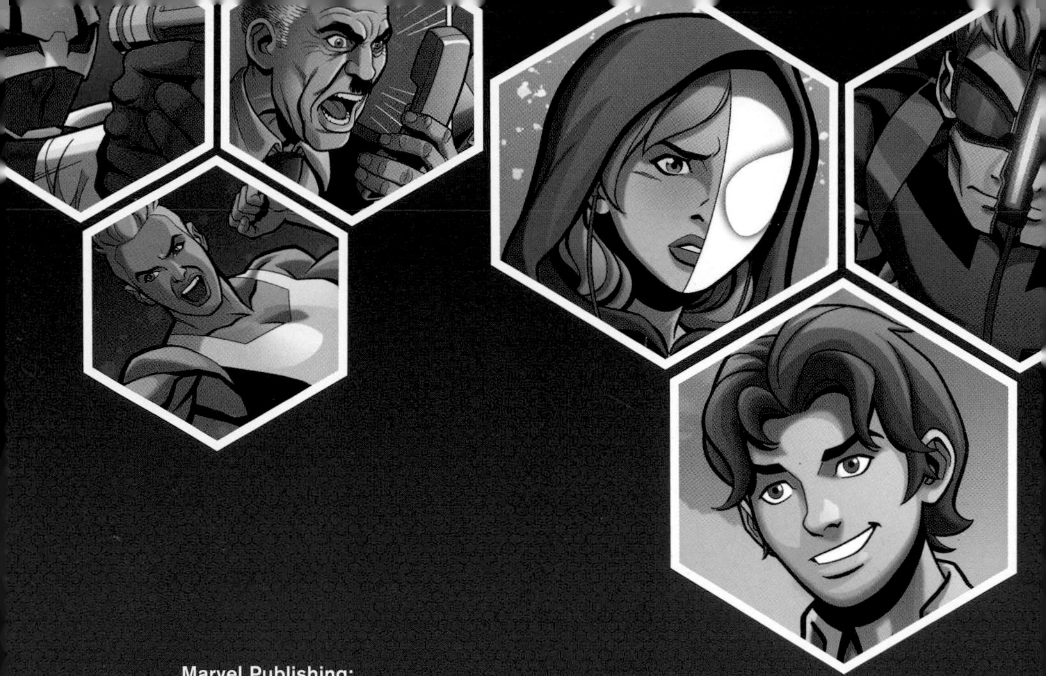

Marvel Publishing:

Jeff Youngquist: VP Production & Special Projects
Caitlin O'Connell: Assistant Editor, Special Projects
Sven Larsen: Director, Licensed Publishing
David Gabriel: SVP Print, Sales & Marketing
C.B. Cebulski: Editor-In-Chief
Joe Quesada: Chief Creative Officer
Dan Buckley: President, Marvel Entertainment
Alan Fine: Executive Producer

IDW Publishing:

Chris Ryall, President, Publisher, & CCO
John Barber, Editor-In-Chief
Cara Morrison, Chief Financial Officer
Matt Ruzicka, Chief Accounting Officer
David Hedgecock, Associate Publisher
Jerry Bennington, VP of New Product Development
Lorelei Bunjes, VP of Digital Services
Justin Eisinger, Editorial Director, Graphic Novels & Collections
Eric Moss, Senior Director, Licensing and Business Development

Ted Adams and **Robbie Robbins**, IDW Founders

Cover Art by
CHRISTOPHER JONES

Cover Colors by
ZAC ATKINSON

Collection Edits
JUSTIN EISINGER
and ALONZO SIMON

Production Assistance
CLAUDIA CHONG

ISBN: 978-1-68405-521-0 22 21 20 19 1 2 3 4

Special thanks: **Nick Lowe**

MARVEL ACTION: SPIDER-MAN: SPIDER-CHASE (BOOK 2). OCTOBER 2019. FIRST PRINTING.

Printed in Korea.

IDW Publishing does not read or accept unsolicited submissions of ideas, stories, or artwork.

Originally published as MARVEL ACTION: SPIDER-MAN issues #4–6.

For international rights, contact licensing@idwpublishing.com

MARVEL

MARVEL ACTION SPIDER-MAN

SPIDER-CHASE

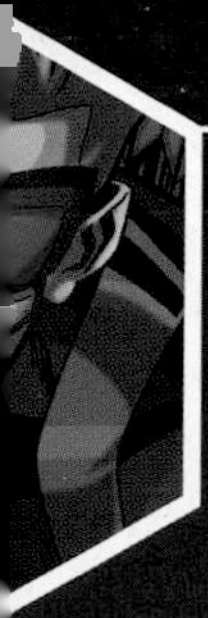

WRITTEN BY ERIK BURNHAM

ART BY CHRISTOPHER JONES

COLORS BY ZAC ATKINSON

LETTERS BY SHAWN LEE

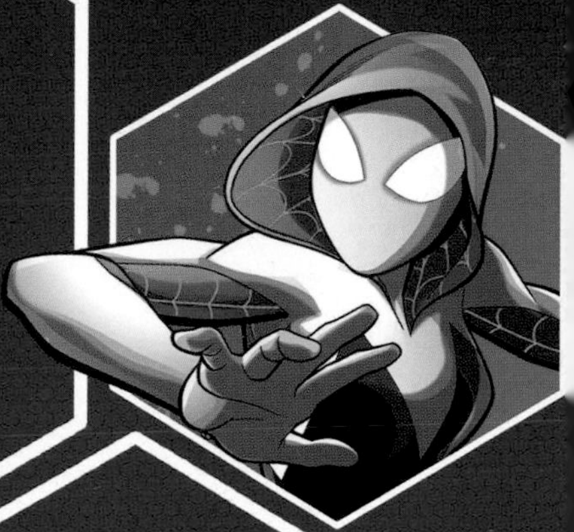

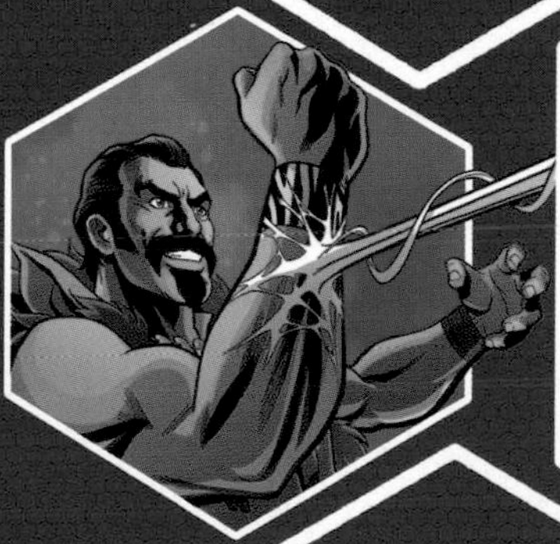

ASSISTANT EDITOR ANNI PERHEENTUPA

ASSOCIATE EDITORS ELIZABETH BREI & CHASE MAROTZ

EDITOR DENTON J. TIPTON

EDITOR-IN-CHIEF JOHN BARBER

SPIDER-MAN CREATED BY STAN LEE & STEVE DITKO

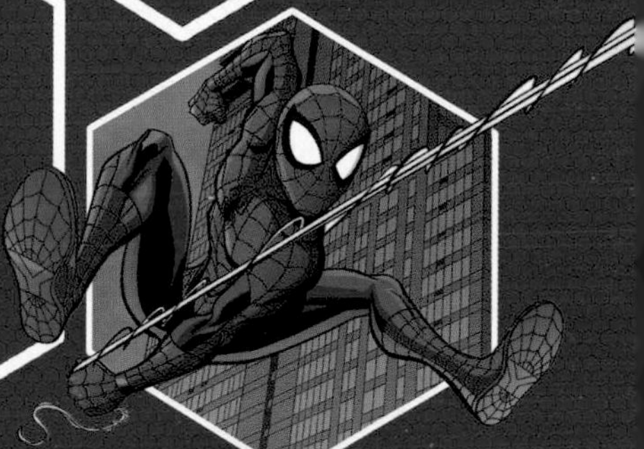

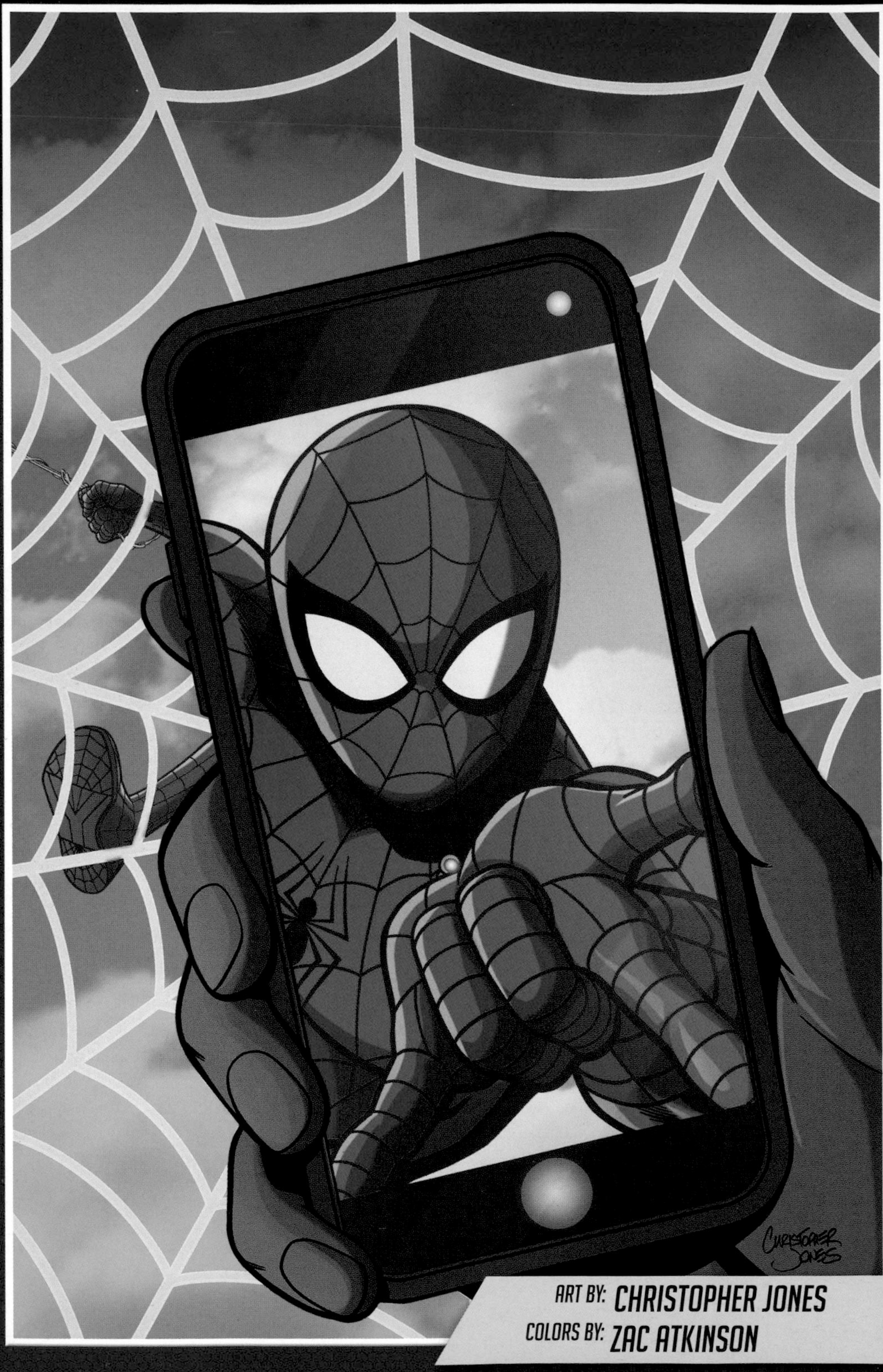
CHRISTOPHER JONES

ART BY: CHRISTOPHER JONES
COLORS BY: ZAC ATKINSON

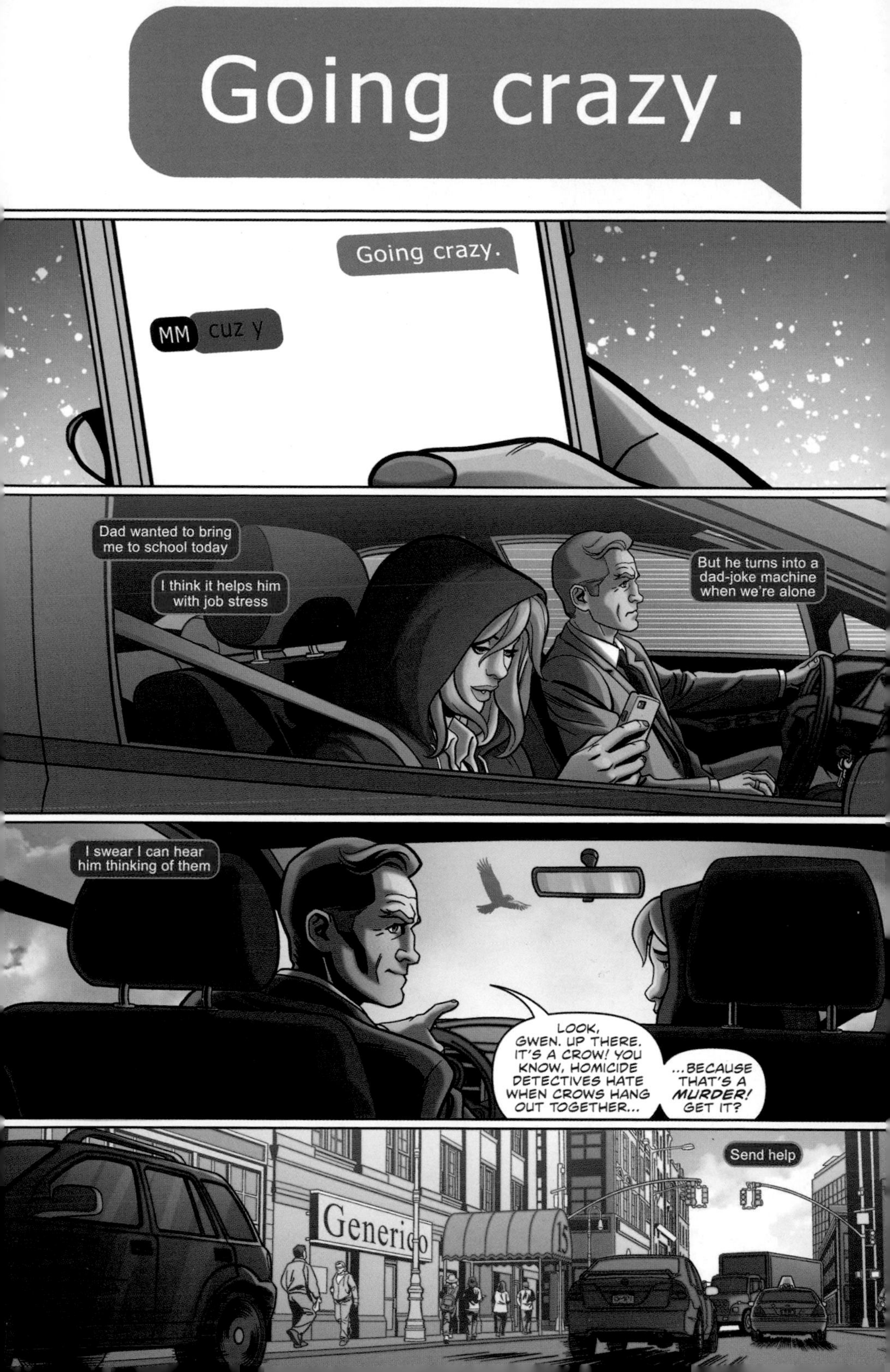
Going crazy.
Going crazy.
MM cuz y
Dad wanted to bring me to school today
I think it helps him with job stress
But he turns into a dad-joke machine when we're alone
I swear I can hear him thinking of them
LOOK, GWEN. UP THERE. IT'S A CROW! YOU KNOW, HOMICIDE DETECTIVES HATE WHEN CROWS HANG OUT TOGETHER...
...BECAUSE THAT'S A *MURDER!* GET IT?
Send help
Generico
15

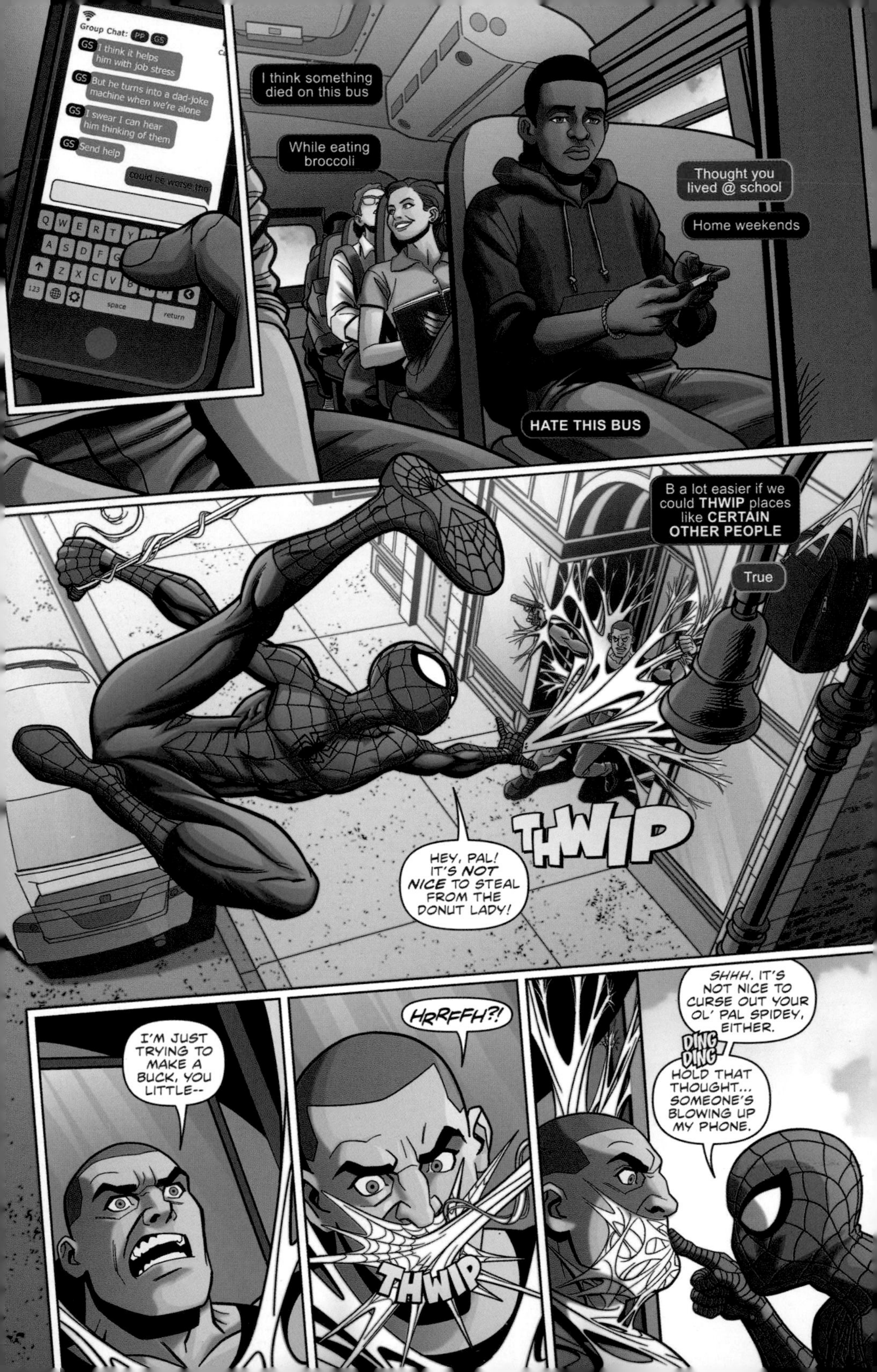
Group Chat: PP GS
GS I think it helps him with job stress
GS But he turns into a dad-joke machine when we're alone
GS I swear I can hear him thinking of them
GS Send help
could be worse tho
I think something died on this bus
While eating broccoli
Thought you lived @ school
Home weekends
HATE THIS BUS
B a lot easier if we could THWIP places like CERTAIN OTHER PEOPLE
True
THWIP
HEY, PAL! IT'S NOT NICE TO STEAL FROM THE DONUT LADY!
I'M JUST TRYING TO MAKE A BUCK, YOU LITTLE--
HRRFFH?!
THWIP
SHHH. IT'S NOT NICE TO CURSE OUT YOUR OL' PAL SPIDEY, EITHER.
DING DING
HOLD THAT THOUGHT... SOMEONE'S BLOWING UP MY PHONE.

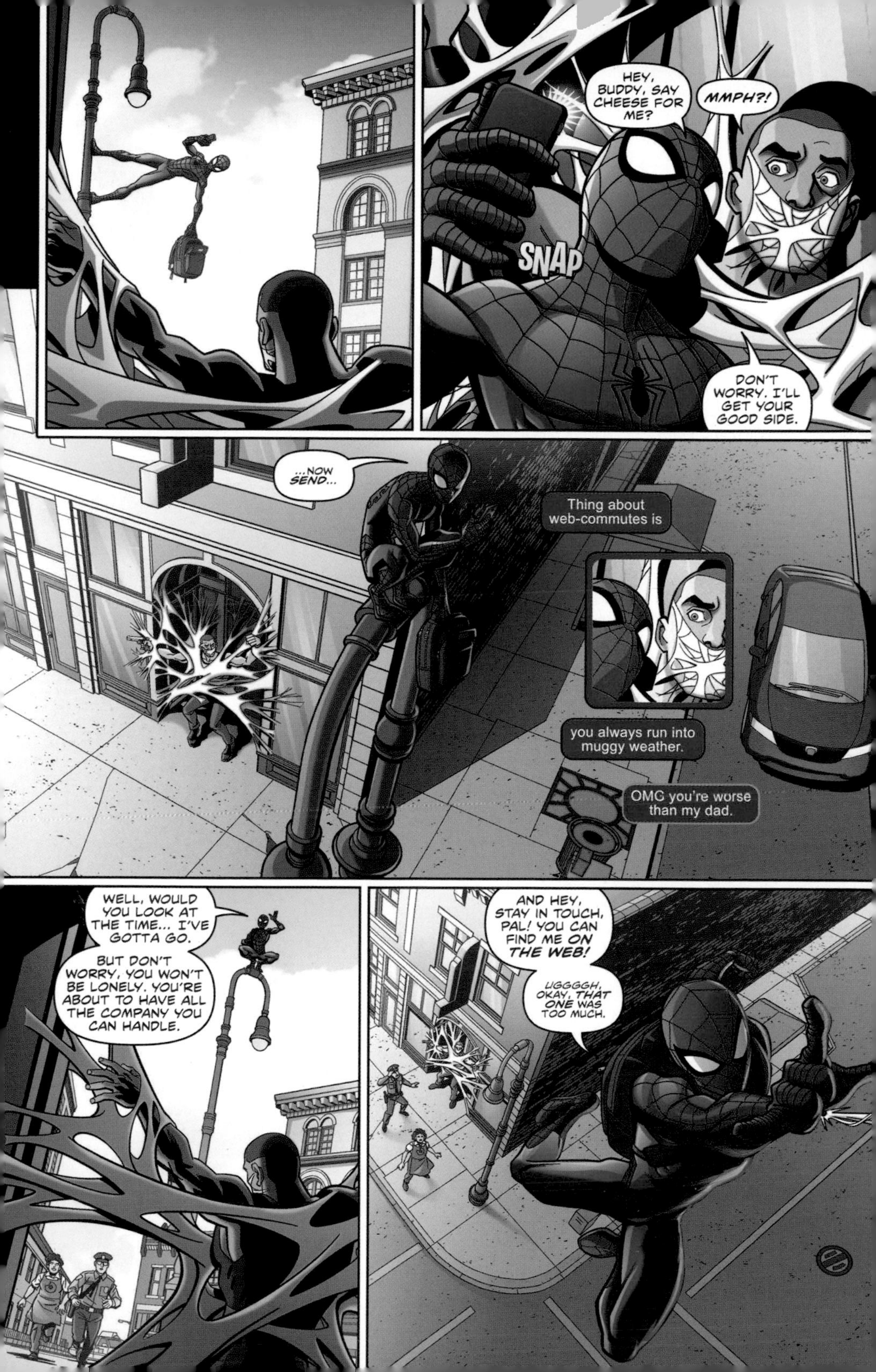
HEY, BUDDY, SAY CHEESE FOR ME?
MMPH?!
SNAP
DON'T WORRY. I'LL GET YOUR GOOD SIDE.
...NOW SEND...
Thing about web-commutes is
you always run into muggy weather.
OMG you're worse than my dad.
WELL, WOULD YOU LOOK AT THE TIME... I'VE GOTTA GO.
BUT DON'T WORRY, YOU WON'T BE LONELY. YOU'RE ABOUT TO HAVE ALL THE COMPANY YOU CAN HANDLE.
AND HEY, STAY IN TOUCH, PAL! YOU CAN FIND ME ON THE WEB!
UGGGGH, OKAY, THAT ONE WAS TOO MUCH.

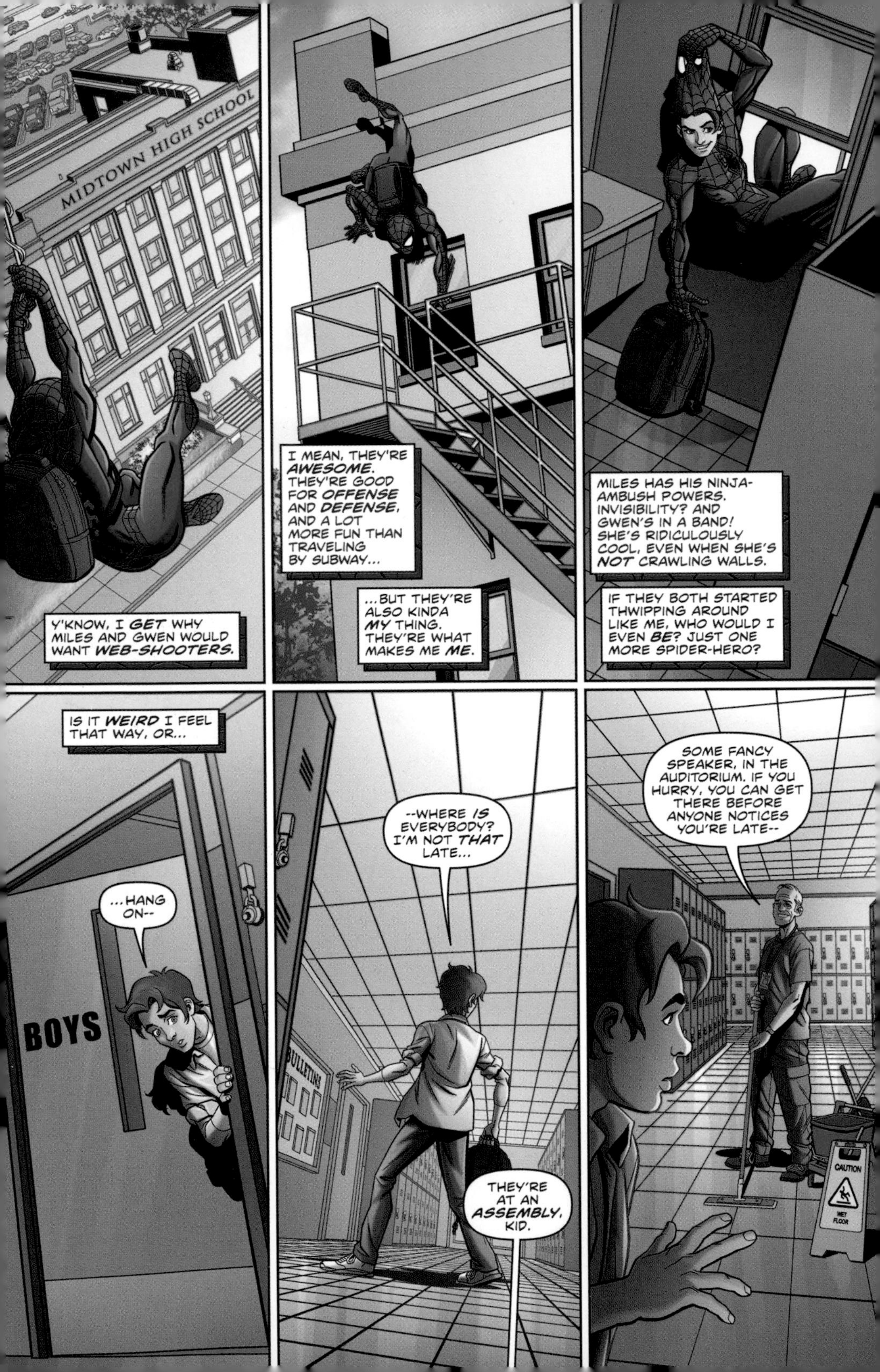
MIDTOWN HIGH SCHOOL
Y'KNOW, I GET WHY MILES AND GWEN WOULD WANT WEB-SHOOTERS.
I MEAN, THEY'RE AWESOME. THEY'RE GOOD FOR OFFENSE AND DEFENSE, AND A LOT MORE FUN THAN TRAVELING BY SUBWAY...
...BUT THEY'RE ALSO KINDA MY THING. THEY'RE WHAT MAKES ME ME.
MILES HAS HIS NINJA-AMBUSH POWERS. INVISIBILITY? AND GWEN'S IN A BAND! SHE'S RIDICULOUSLY COOL, EVEN WHEN SHE'S NOT CRAWLING WALLS.
IF THEY BOTH STARTED THWIPPING AROUND LIKE ME, WHO WOULD I EVEN BE? JUST ONE MORE SPIDER-HERO?
IS IT WEIRD I FEEL THAT WAY, OR...
...HANG ON--
BOYS
--WHERE IS EVERYBODY? I'M NOT THAT LATE...
BULLETINS
THEY'RE AT AN ASSEMBLY, KID.
SOME FANCY SPEAKER, IN THE AUDITORIUM. IF YOU HURRY, YOU CAN GET THERE BEFORE ANYONE NOTICES YOU'RE LATE--
CAUTION
WET FLOOR

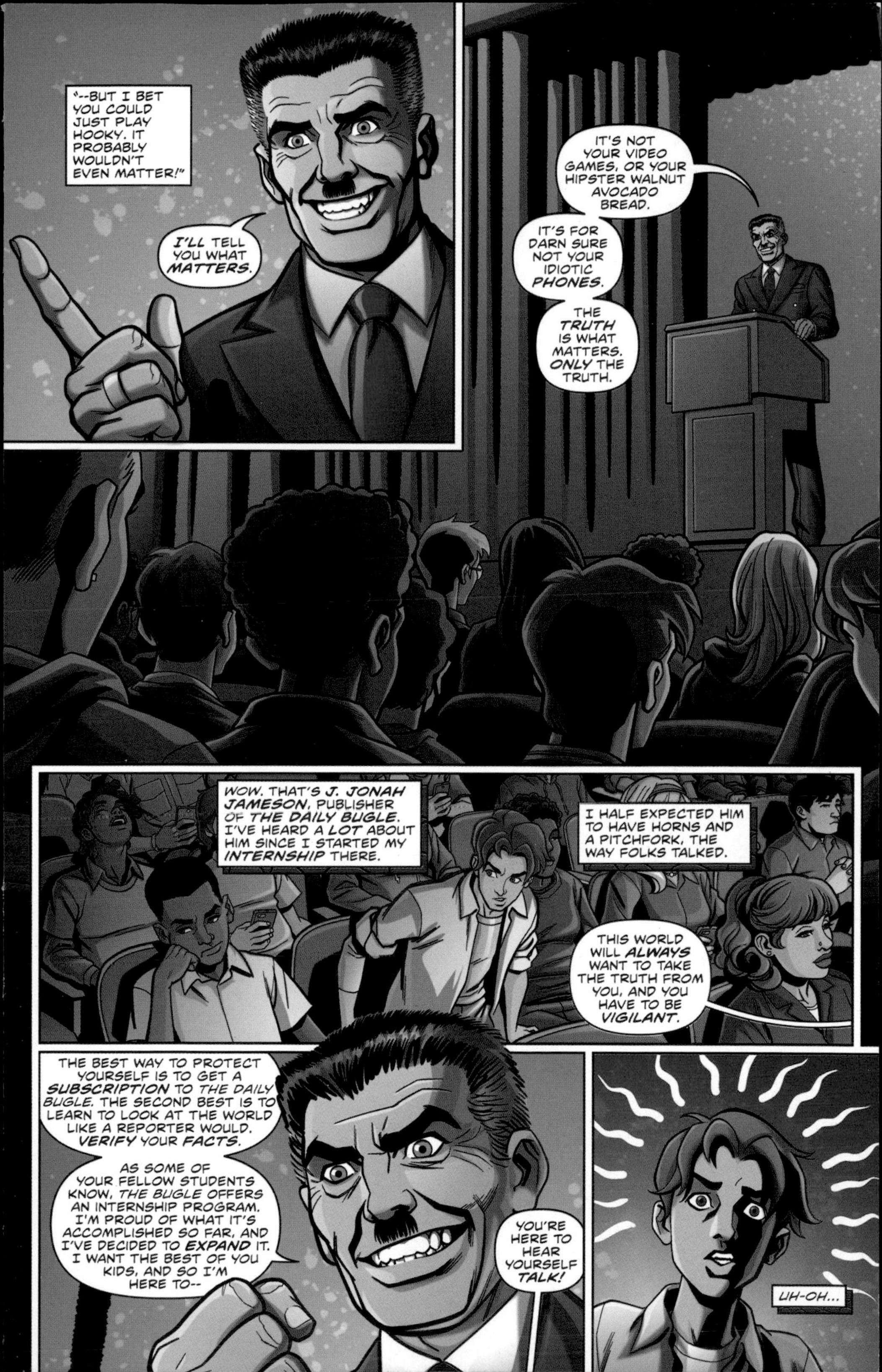
"--BUT I BET YOU COULD JUST PLAY HOOKY. IT PROBABLY WOULDN'T EVEN MATTER!"
I'LL TELL YOU WHAT MATTERS.
IT'S NOT YOUR VIDEO GAMES, OR YOUR HIPSTER WALNUT AVOCADO BREAD.
IT'S FOR DARN SURE NOT YOUR IDIOTIC PHONES.
THE TRUTH IS WHAT MATTERS. ONLY THE TRUTH.
WOW. THAT'S J. JONAH JAMESON, PUBLISHER OF THE DAILY BUGLE. I'VE HEARD A LOT ABOUT HIM SINCE I STARTED MY INTERNSHIP THERE.
I HALF EXPECTED HIM TO HAVE HORNS AND A PITCHFORK, THE WAY FOLKS TALKED.
THIS WORLD WILL ALWAYS WANT TO TAKE THE TRUTH FROM YOU, AND YOU HAVE TO BE VIGILANT.
THE BEST WAY TO PROTECT YOURSELF IS TO GET A SUBSCRIPTION TO THE DAILY BUGLE. THE SECOND BEST IS TO LEARN TO LOOK AT THE WORLD LIKE A REPORTER WOULD. VERIFY YOUR FACTS.
AS SOME OF YOUR FELLOW STUDENTS KNOW, THE BUGLE OFFERS AN INTERNSHIP PROGRAM. I'M PROUD OF WHAT IT'S ACCOMPLISHED SO FAR, AND I'VE DECIDED TO EXPAND IT. I WANT THE BEST OF YOU KIDS, AND SO I'M HERE TO--
YOU'RE HERE TO HEAR YOURSELF TALK!
UH-OH...

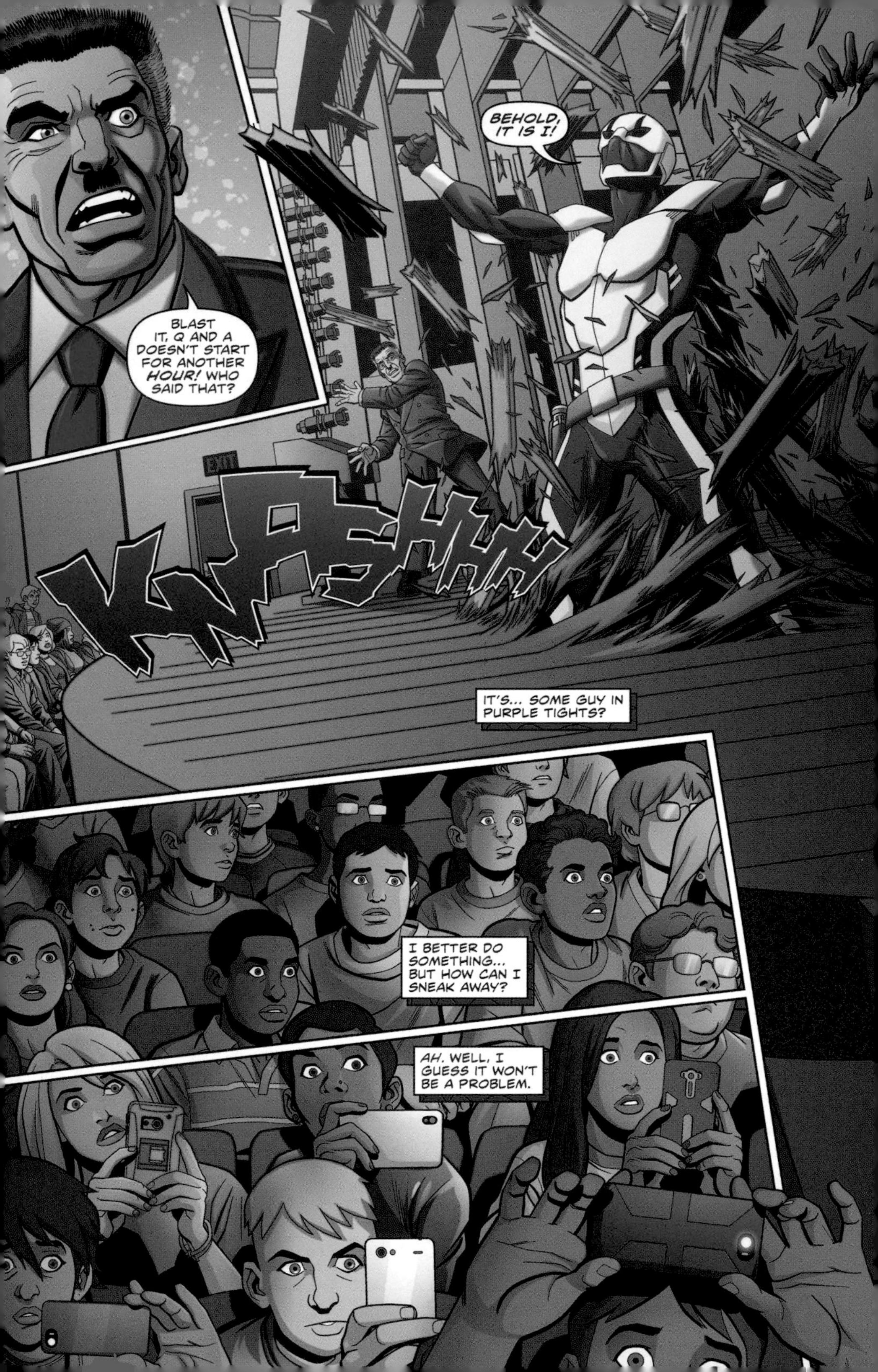
BLAST IT, Q AND A DOESN'T START FOR ANOTHER HOUR! WHO SAID THAT?
BEHOLD, IT IS I!
KRASHHH
IT'S... SOME GUY IN PURPLE TIGHTS?
EXIT
I BETTER DO SOMETHING... BUT HOW CAN I SNEAK AWAY?
AH. WELL, I GUESS IT WON'T BE A PROBLEM.

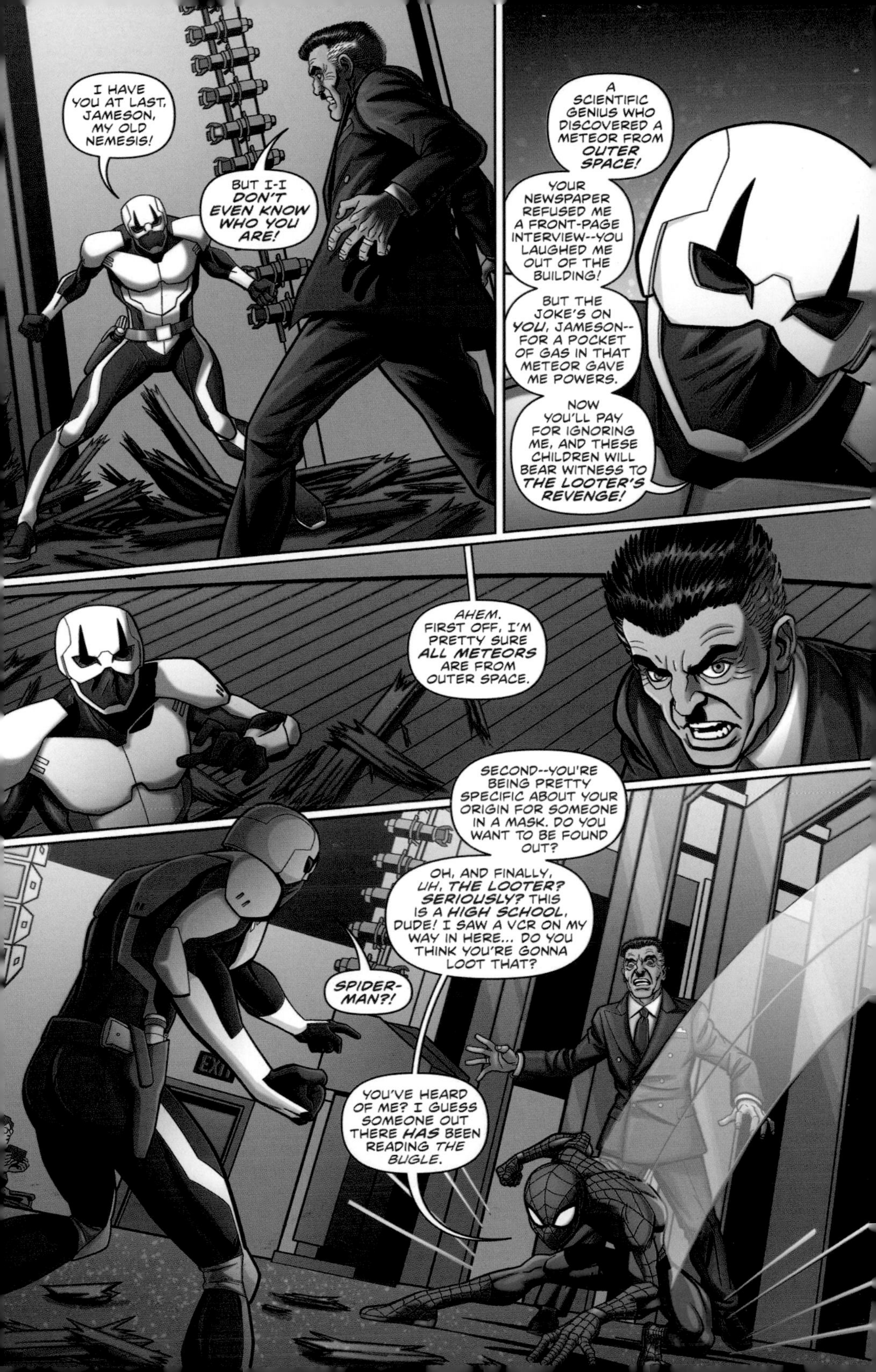
I HAVE YOU AT LAST, JAMESON, MY OLD NEMESIS!
BUT I-I DON'T EVEN KNOW WHO YOU ARE!
A SCIENTIFIC GENIUS WHO DISCOVERED A METEOR FROM OUTER SPACE!
YOUR NEWSPAPER REFUSED ME A FRONT-PAGE INTERVIEW--YOU LAUGHED ME OUT OF THE BUILDING!
BUT THE JOKE'S ON YOU, JAMESON--FOR A POCKET OF GAS IN THAT METEOR GAVE ME POWERS.
NOW YOU'LL PAY FOR IGNORING ME, AND THESE CHILDREN WILL BEAR WITNESS TO THE LOOTER'S REVENGE!
AHEM. FIRST OFF, I'M PRETTY SURE ALL METEORS ARE FROM OUTER SPACE.
SECOND--YOU'RE BEING PRETTY SPECIFIC ABOUT YOUR ORIGIN FOR SOMEONE IN A MASK. DO YOU WANT TO BE FOUND OUT?
OH, AND FINALLY, UH, THE LOOTER? SERIOUSLY? THIS IS A HIGH SCHOOL, DUDE! I SAW A VCR ON MY WAY IN HERE... DO YOU THINK YOU'RE GONNA LOOT THAT?
SPIDER-MAN?!
YOU'VE HEARD OF ME? I GUESS SOMEONE OUT THERE HAS BEEN READING THE BUGLE.
EXIT

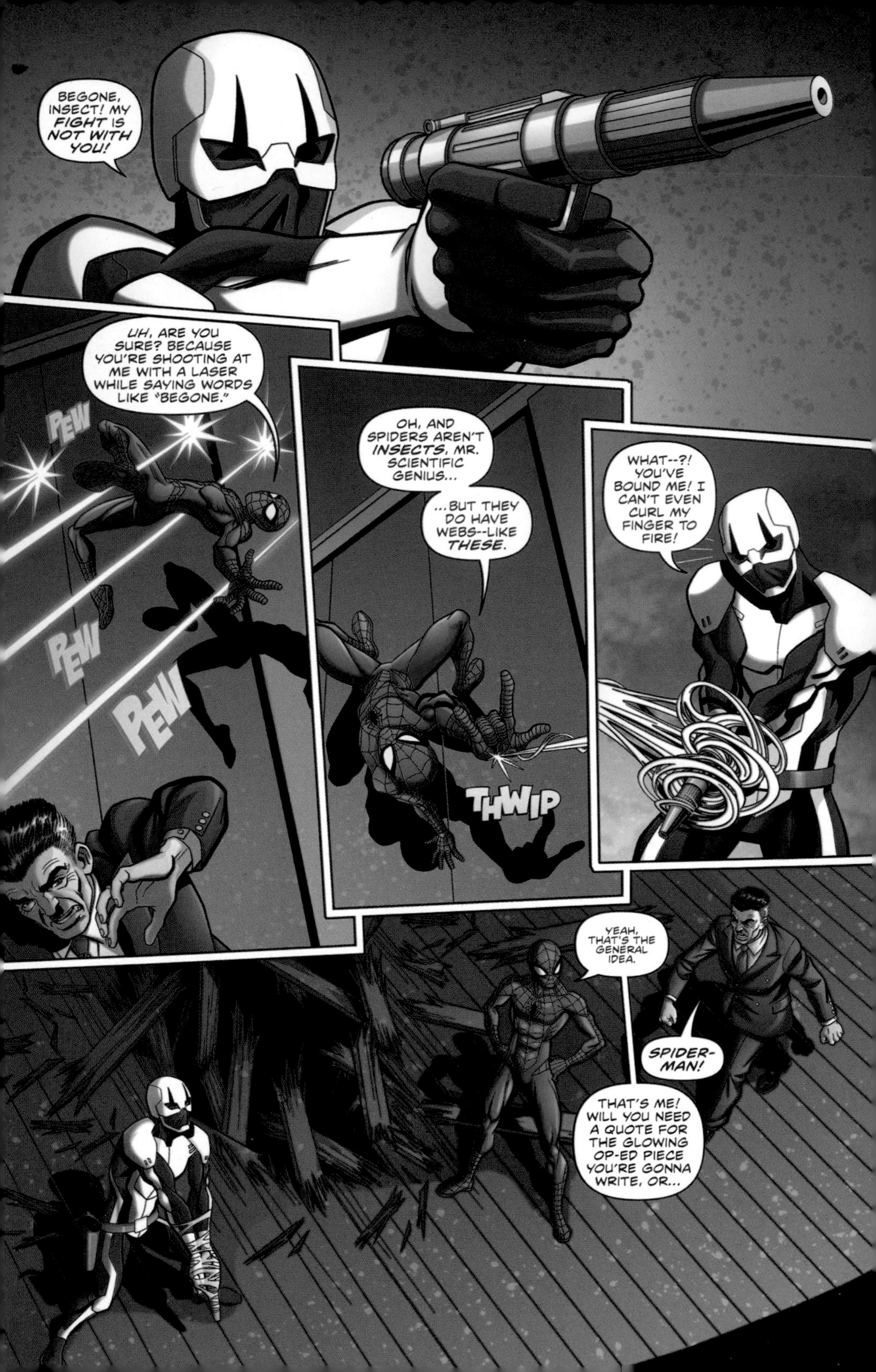
BEGONE, INSECT! MY FIGHT IS NOT WITH YOU!
UH, ARE YOU SURE? BECAUSE YOU'RE SHOOTING AT ME WITH A LASER WHILE SAYING WORDS LIKE "BEGONE."
PEW
PEW
PEW
OH, AND SPIDERS AREN'T INSECTS, MR. SCIENTIFIC GENIUS...
...BUT THEY DO HAVE WEBS--LIKE THESE.
THWIP
WHAT--?! YOU'VE BOUND ME! I CAN'T EVEN CURL MY FINGER TO FIRE!
SPIDER-MAN!
YEAH, THAT'S THE GENERAL IDEA.
THAT'S ME! WILL YOU NEED A QUOTE FOR THE GLOWING OP-ED PIECE YOU'RE GONNA WRITE, OR...

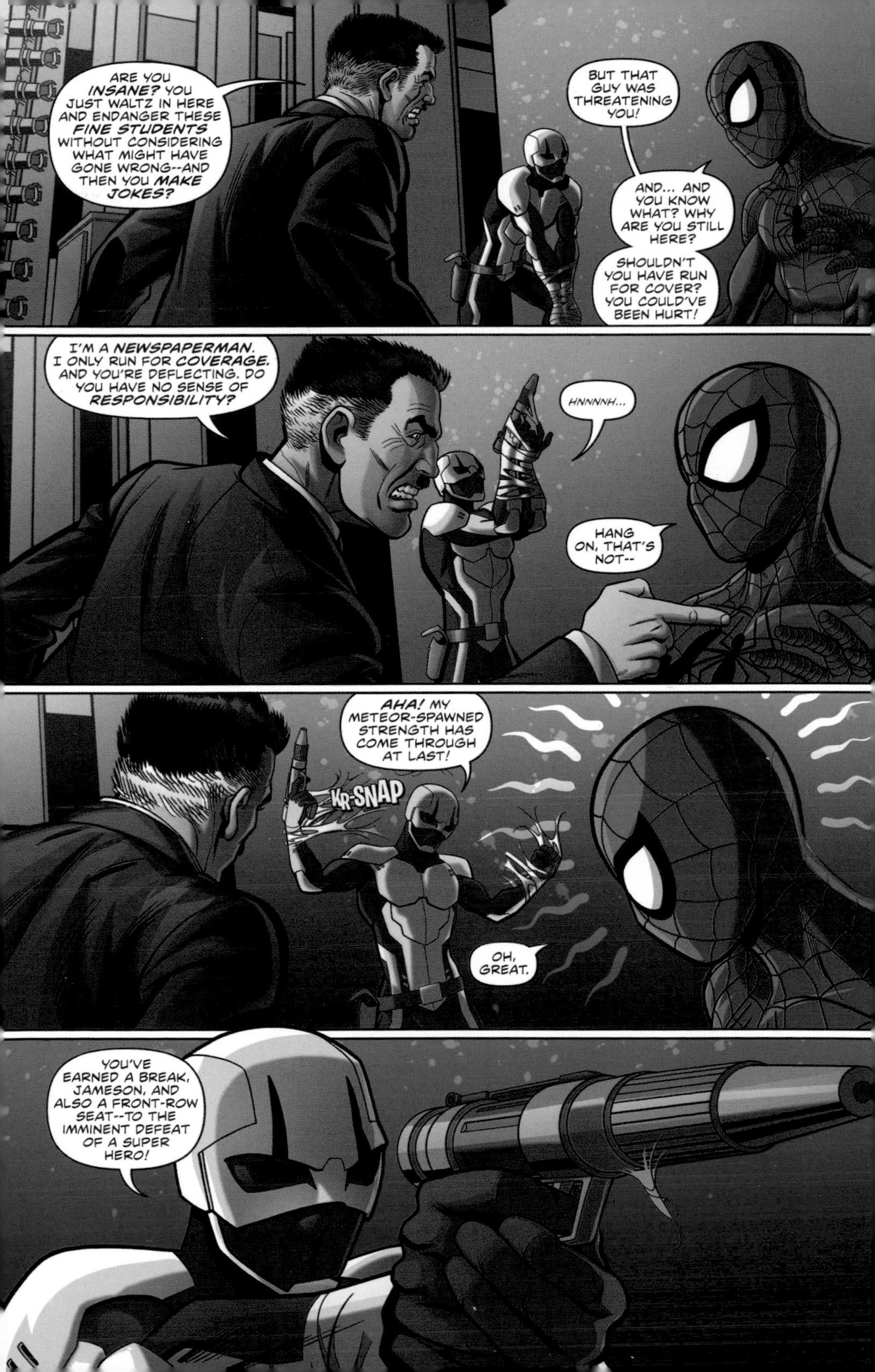
ARE YOU INSANE? YOU JUST WALTZ IN HERE AND ENDANGER THESE FINE STUDENTS WITHOUT CONSIDERING WHAT MIGHT HAVE GONE WRONG--AND THEN YOU MAKE JOKES?
BUT THAT GUY WAS THREATENING YOU!
AND... AND YOU KNOW WHAT? WHY ARE YOU STILL HERE?
SHOULDN'T YOU HAVE RUN FOR COVER? YOU COULD'VE BEEN HURT!
I'M A NEWSPAPERMAN. I ONLY RUN FOR COVERAGE. AND YOU'RE DEFLECTING. DO YOU HAVE NO SENSE OF RESPONSIBILITY?
HNNNNH...
HANG ON, THAT'S NOT--
AHA! MY METEOR-SPAWNED STRENGTH HAS COME THROUGH AT LAST!
KR-SNAP
OH, GREAT.
YOU'VE EARNED A BREAK, JAMESON, AND ALSO A FRONT-ROW SEAT--TO THE IMMINENT DEFEAT OF A SUPER HERO!

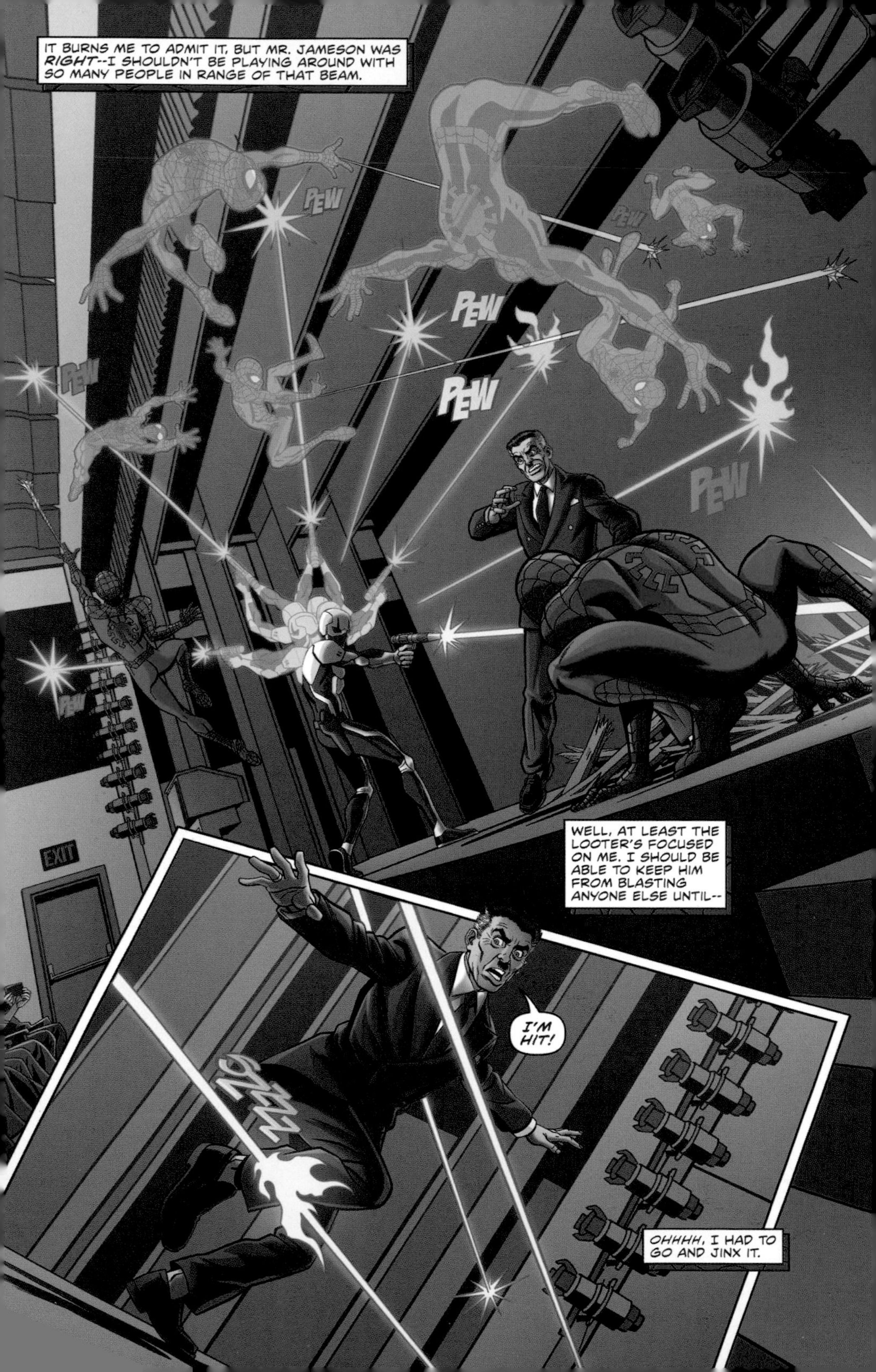
IT BURNS ME TO ADMIT IT, BUT MR. JAMESON WAS RIGHT--I SHOULDN'T BE PLAYING AROUND WITH SO MANY PEOPLE IN RANGE OF THAT BEAM.
PEW
PEW
PEW
PEW
PEW
PEW
PEW
WELL, AT LEAST THE LOOTER'S FOCUSED ON ME. I SHOULD BE ABLE TO KEEP HIM FROM BLASTING ANYONE ELSE UNTIL--
I'M HIT!
ZZZAG
OHHHH, I HAD TO GO AND JINX IT.

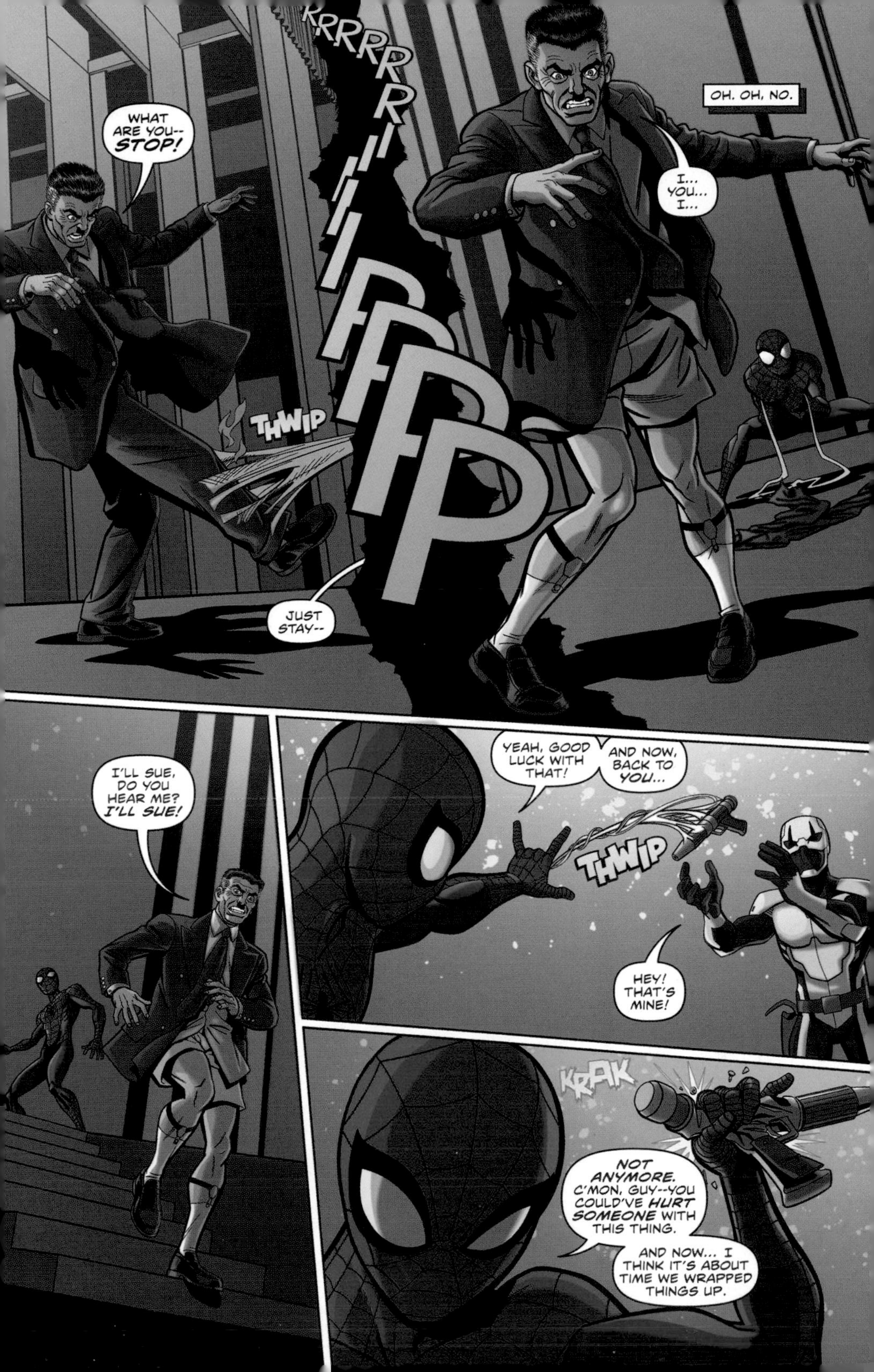
KRRRRRR
OH. OH, NO.
WHAT ARE YOU-- STOP!
I... YOU... I...
IIIIIIPPPP
THWIP
JUST STAY--
I'LL SUE, DO YOU HEAR ME? I'LL SUE!
YEAH, GOOD LUCK WITH THAT!
AND NOW, BACK TO YOU...
THWIP
HEY! THAT'S MINE!
KRAK
NOT ANYMORE. C'MON, GUY--YOU COULD'VE HURT SOMEONE WITH THIS THING.
AND NOW... I THINK IT'S ABOUT TIME WE WRAPPED THINGS UP.

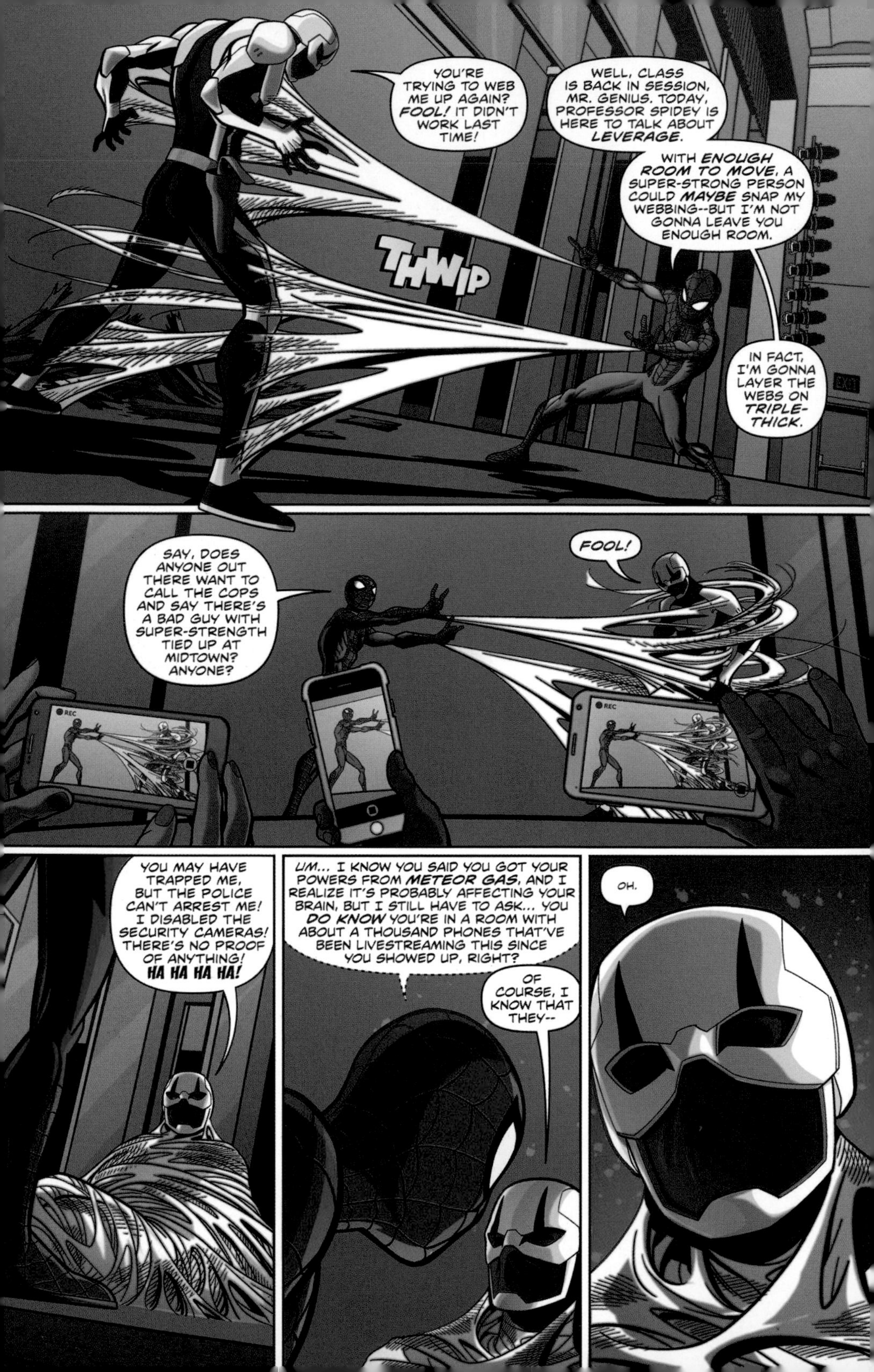
YOU'RE TRYING TO WEB ME UP AGAIN? *FOOL!* IT DIDN'T WORK LAST TIME!
WELL, CLASS IS BACK IN SESSION, MR. GENIUS. TODAY, PROFESSOR SPIDEY IS HERE TO TALK ABOUT *LEVERAGE*.
WITH *ENOUGH ROOM TO MOVE*, A SUPER-STRONG PERSON COULD *MAYBE* SNAP MY WEBBING--BUT I'M NOT GONNA LEAVE YOU ENOUGH ROOM.
THWIP
IN FACT, I'M GONNA LAYER THE WEBS ON *TRIPLE-THICK*.
EXIT
SAY, DOES ANYONE OUT THERE WANT TO CALL THE COPS AND SAY THERE'S A BAD GUY WITH SUPER-STRENGTH TIED UP AT MIDTOWN? ANYONE?
FOOL!
REC
REC
YOU MAY HAVE TRAPPED ME, BUT THE POLICE CAN'T ARREST ME! I DISABLED THE SECURITY CAMERAS! THERE'S NO PROOF OF ANYTHING! **HA HA HA HA!**
UM... I KNOW YOU SAID YOU GOT YOUR POWERS FROM *METEOR GAS*, AND I REALIZE IT'S PROBABLY AFFECTING YOUR BRAIN, BUT I STILL HAVE TO ASK... YOU *DO KNOW* YOU'RE IN A ROOM WITH ABOUT A THOUSAND PHONES THAT'VE BEEN LIVESTREAMING THIS SINCE YOU SHOWED UP, RIGHT?
OF COURSE, I KNOW THAT THEY--
OH.

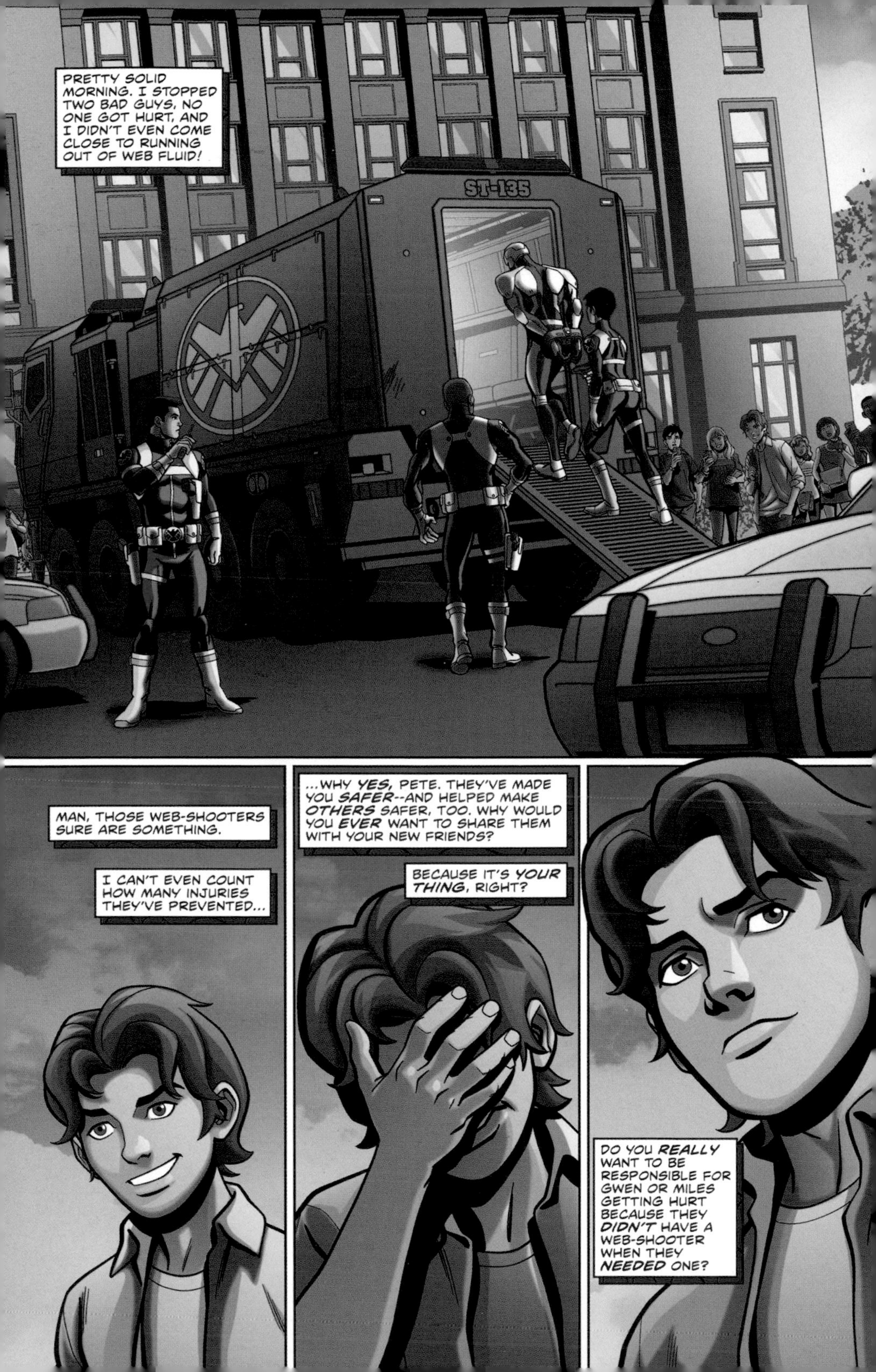
PRETTY SOLID MORNING. I STOPPED TWO BAD GUYS, NO ONE GOT HURT, AND I DIDN'T EVEN COME CLOSE TO RUNNING OUT OF WEB FLUID!
ST-135
MAN, THOSE WEB-SHOOTERS SURE ARE SOMETHING.
I CAN'T EVEN COUNT HOW MANY INJURIES THEY'VE PREVENTED...
...WHY YES, PETE. THEY'VE MADE YOU SAFER--AND HELPED MAKE OTHERS SAFER, TOO. WHY WOULD YOU EVER WANT TO SHARE THEM WITH YOUR NEW FRIENDS?
BECAUSE IT'S YOUR THING, RIGHT?
DO YOU REALLY WANT TO BE RESPONSIBLE FOR GWEN OR MILES GETTING HURT BECAUSE THEY DIDN'T HAVE A WEB-SHOOTER WHEN THEY NEEDED ONE?

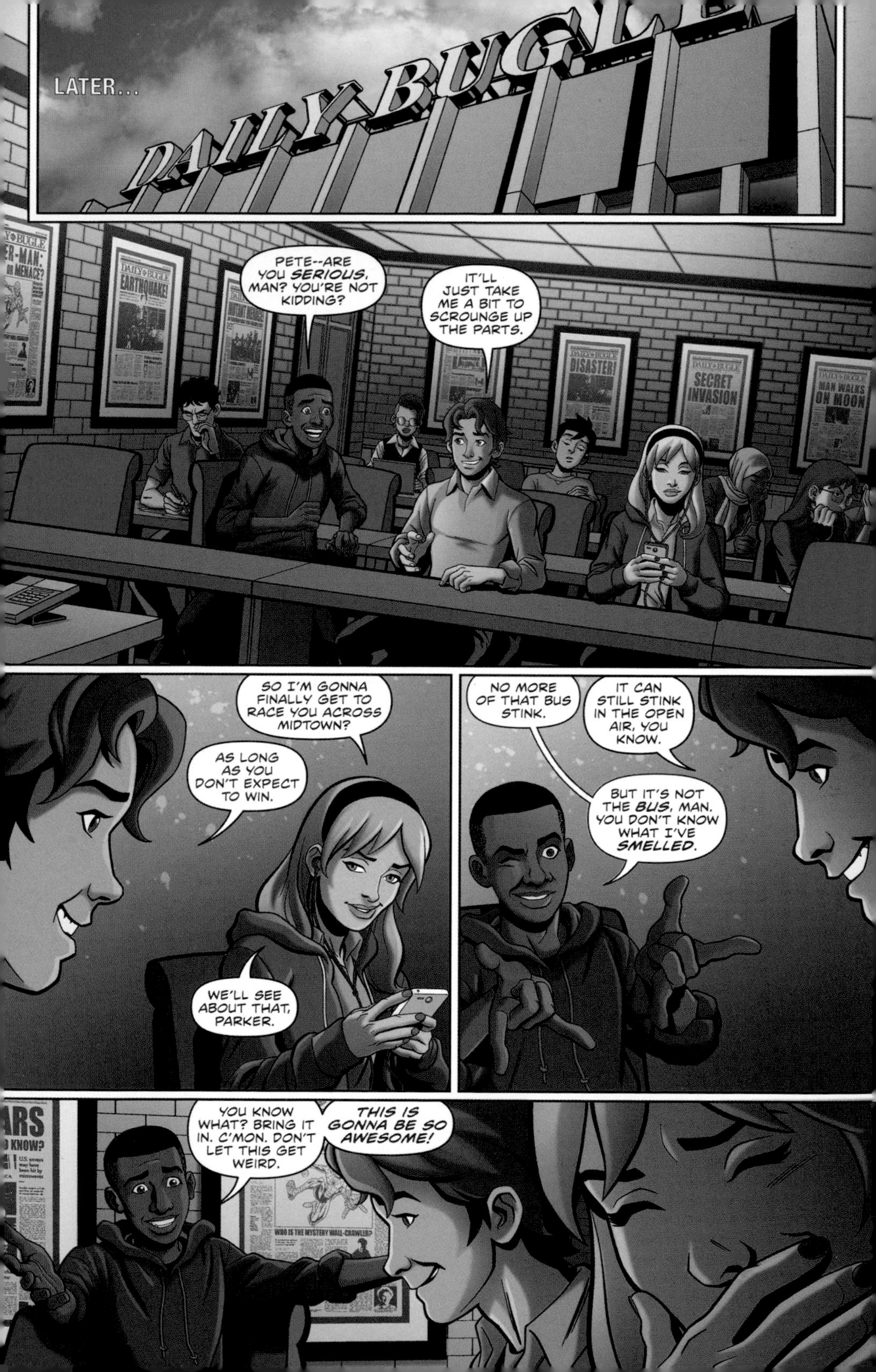

LATER...
DAILY BUGLE
PETE--ARE YOU SERIOUS, MAN? YOU'RE NOT KIDDING?
IT'LL JUST TAKE ME A BIT TO SCROUNGE UP THE PARTS.
SO I'M GONNA FINALLY GET TO RACE YOU ACROSS MIDTOWN?
AS LONG AS YOU DON'T EXPECT TO WIN.
WE'LL SEE ABOUT THAT, PARKER.
NO MORE OF THAT BUS STINK.
IT CAN STILL STINK IN THE OPEN AIR, YOU KNOW.
BUT IT'S NOT THE BUS, MAN. YOU DON'T KNOW WHAT I'VE SMELLED.
YOU KNOW WHAT? BRING IT IN. C'MON. DON'T LET THIS GET WEIRD.
THIS IS GONNA BE SO AWESOME!

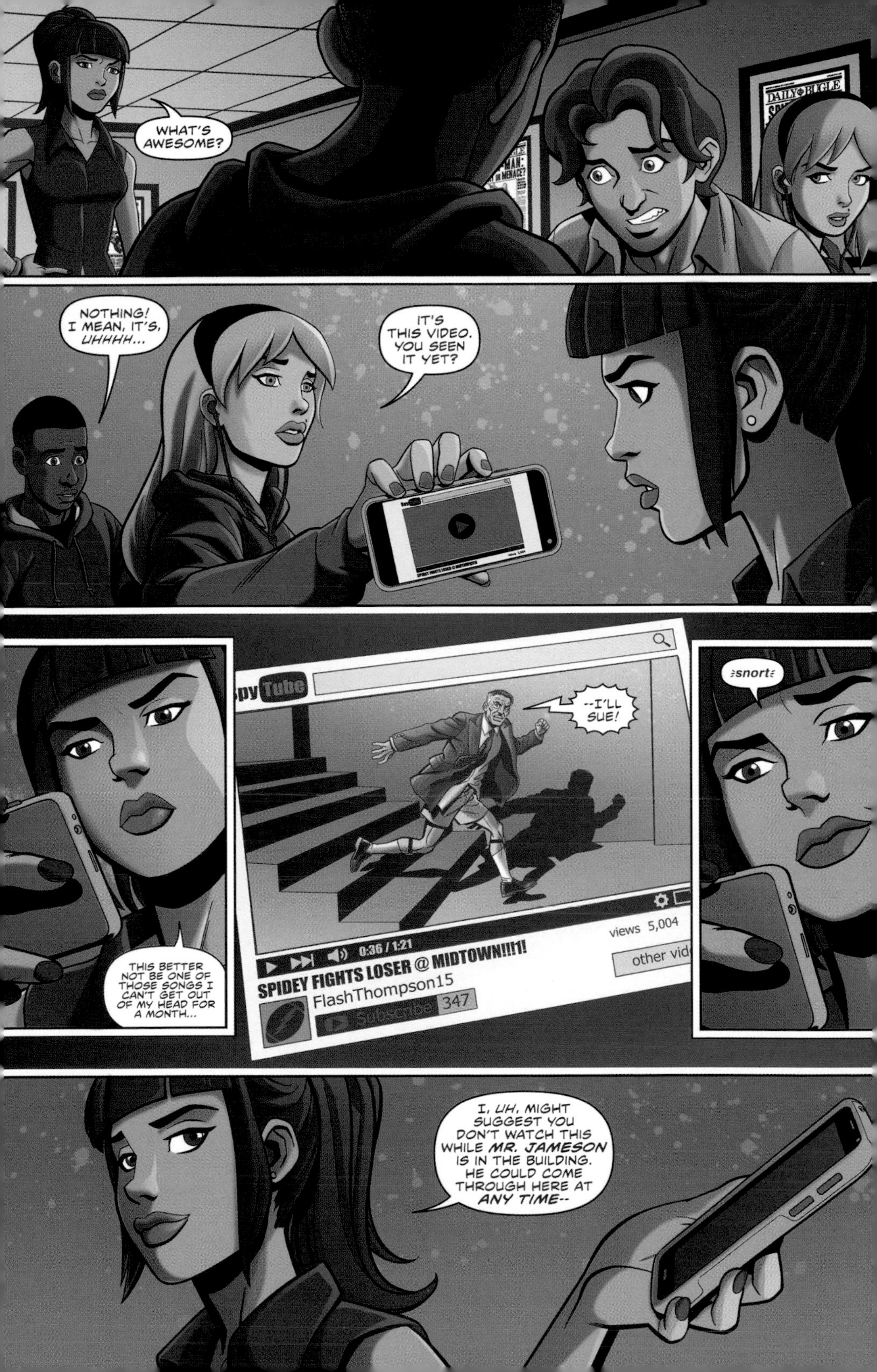

DAILY BUGLE
WHAT'S AWESOME?
NOTHING! I MEAN, IT'S, *UHHHH*...
IT'S THIS VIDEO. YOU SEEN IT YET?
THIS BETTER NOT BE ONE OF THOSE SONGS I CAN'T GET OUT OF MY HEAD FOR A MONTH...
SpyTube
--I'LL SUE!
0:36 / 1:21
SPIDEY FIGHTS LOSER @ MIDTOWN!!!1!
FlashThompson15
Subscribe 347
views 5,004
snort
I, *UH*, MIGHT SUGGEST YOU DON'T WATCH THIS WHILE ***MR. JAMESON*** IS IN THE BUILDING. HE COULD COME THROUGH HERE AT ***ANY TIME***--

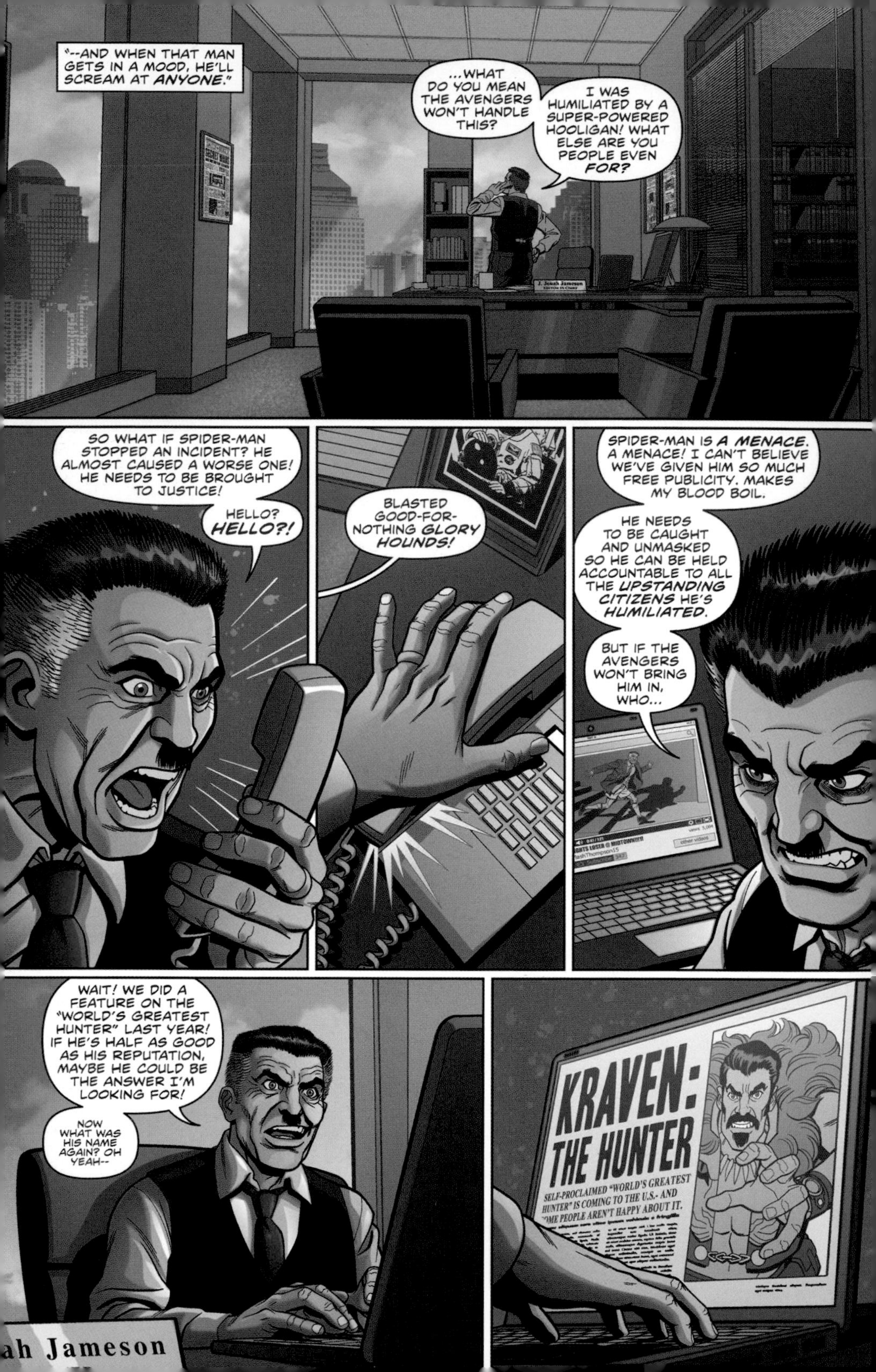
"--AND WHEN THAT MAN GETS IN A MOOD, HE'LL SCREAM AT ANYONE."
...WHAT DO YOU MEAN THE AVENGERS WON'T HANDLE THIS?
I WAS HUMILIATED BY A SUPER-POWERED HOOLIGAN! WHAT ELSE ARE YOU PEOPLE EVEN FOR?
J. Jonah Jameson
SO WHAT IF SPIDER-MAN STOPPED AN INCIDENT? HE ALMOST CAUSED A WORSE ONE! HE NEEDS TO BE BROUGHT TO JUSTICE!
HELLO? HELLO?!
BLASTED GOOD-FOR-NOTHING GLORY HOUNDS!
SPIDER-MAN IS A MENACE. A MENACE! I CAN'T BELIEVE WE'VE GIVEN HIM SO MUCH FREE PUBLICITY. MAKES MY BLOOD BOIL.
HE NEEDS TO BE CAUGHT AND UNMASKED SO HE CAN BE HELD ACCOUNTABLE TO ALL THE UPSTANDING CITIZENS HE'S HUMILIATED.
BUT IF THE AVENGERS WON'T BRING HIM IN, WHO...
WAIT! WE DID A FEATURE ON THE "WORLD'S GREATEST HUNTER" LAST YEAR! IF HE'S HALF AS GOOD AS HIS REPUTATION, MAYBE HE COULD BE THE ANSWER I'M LOOKING FOR!
NOW WHAT WAS HIS NAME AGAIN? OH YEAH--
ah Jameson
KRAVEN: THE HUNTER
SELF-PROCLAIMED "WORLD'S GREATEST HUNTER" IS COMING TO THE U.S.- AND SOME PEOPLE AREN'T HAPPY ABOUT IT.

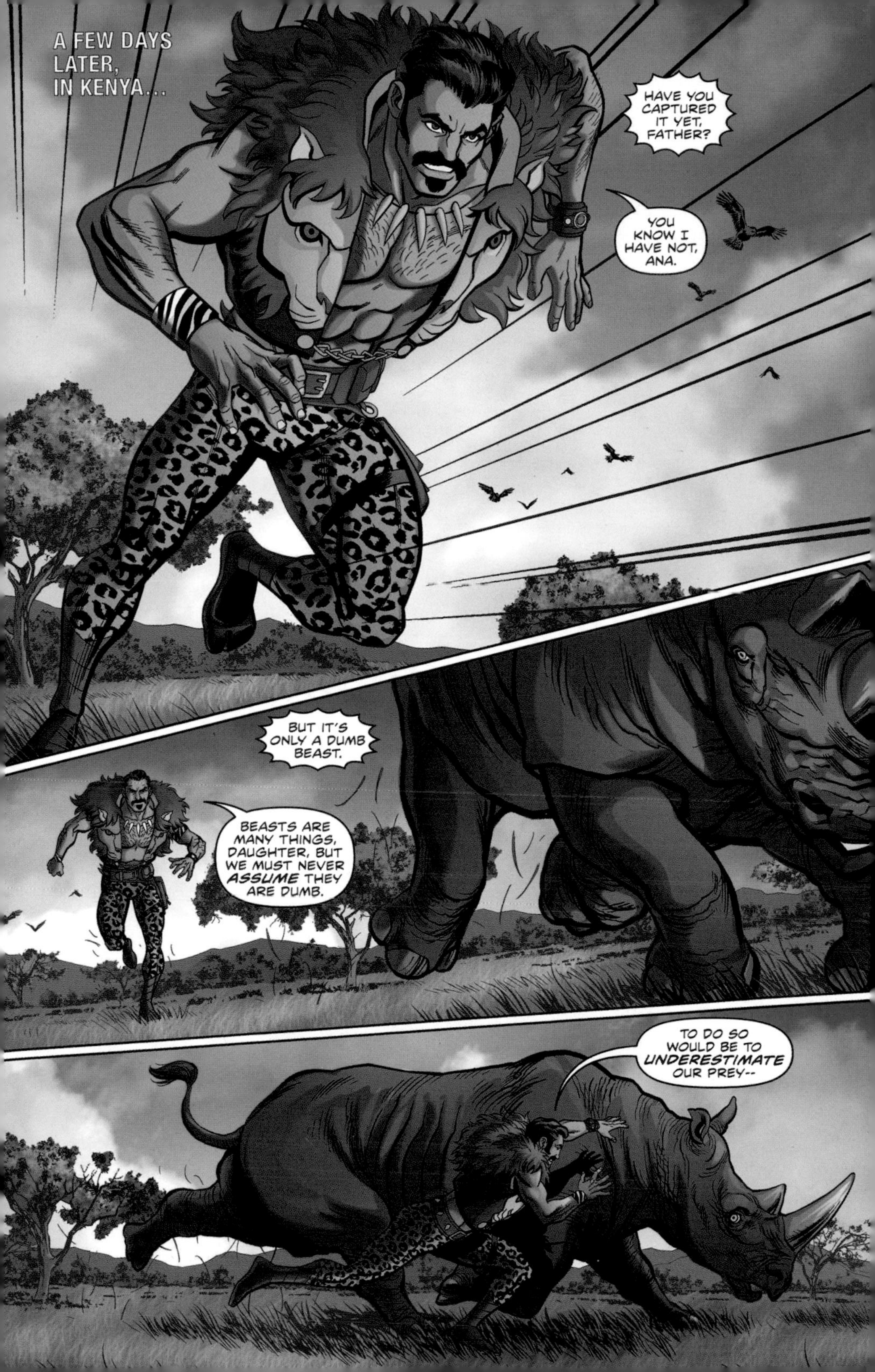
A FEW DAYS LATER, IN KENYA...
HAVE YOU CAPTURED IT YET, FATHER?
YOU KNOW I HAVE NOT, ANA.
BUT IT'S ONLY A DUMB BEAST.
BEASTS ARE MANY THINGS, DAUGHTER, BUT WE MUST NEVER ASSUME THEY ARE DUMB.
TO DO SO WOULD BE TO UNDERESTIMATE OUR PREY--

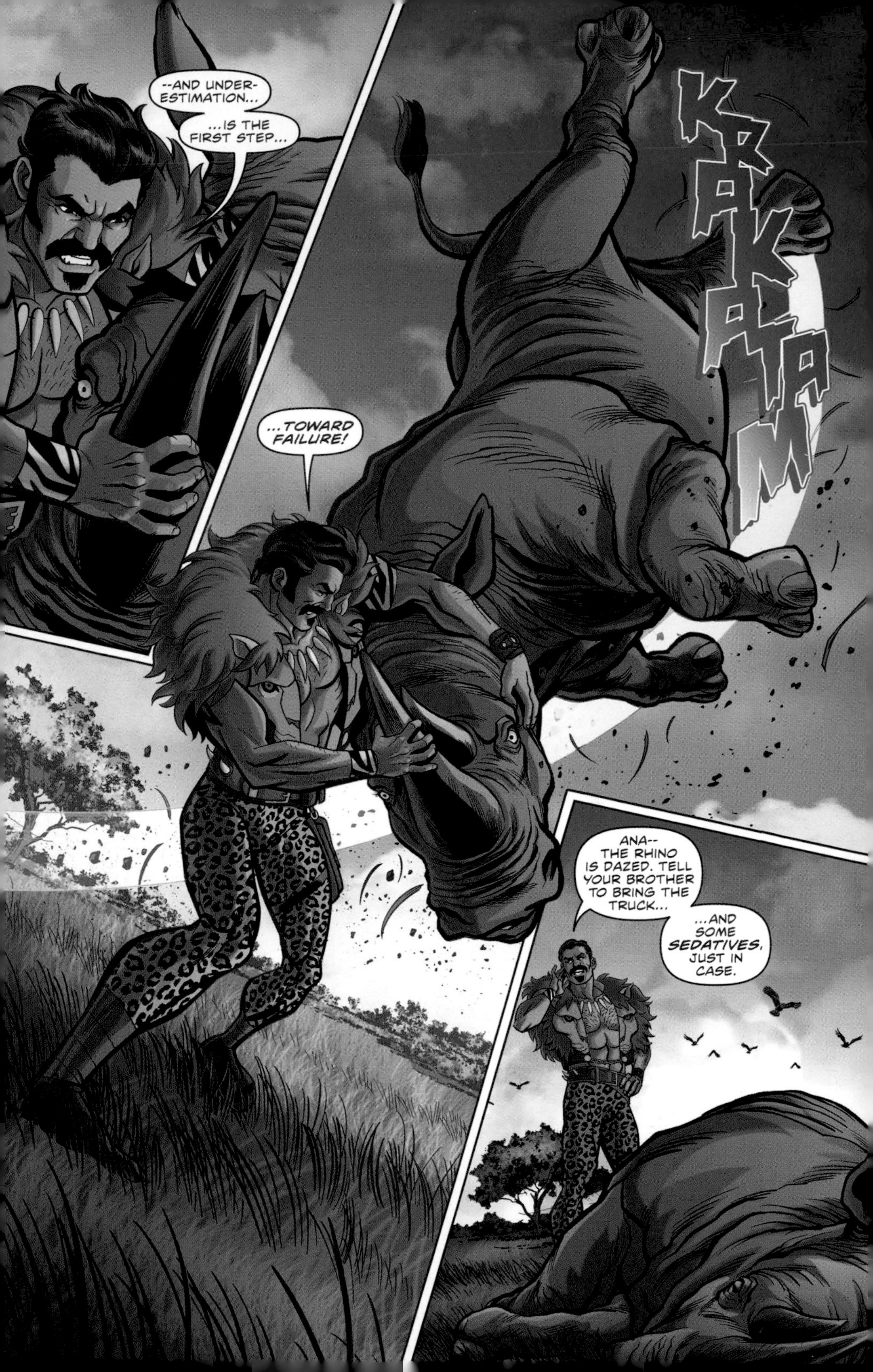
--AND UNDER-ESTIMATION...
...IS THE FIRST STEP...
...TOWARD FAILURE!
KRAKATHAM
ANA-- THE RHINO IS DAZED. TELL YOUR BROTHER TO BRING THE TRUCK...
...AND SOME SEDATIVES, JUST IN CASE.

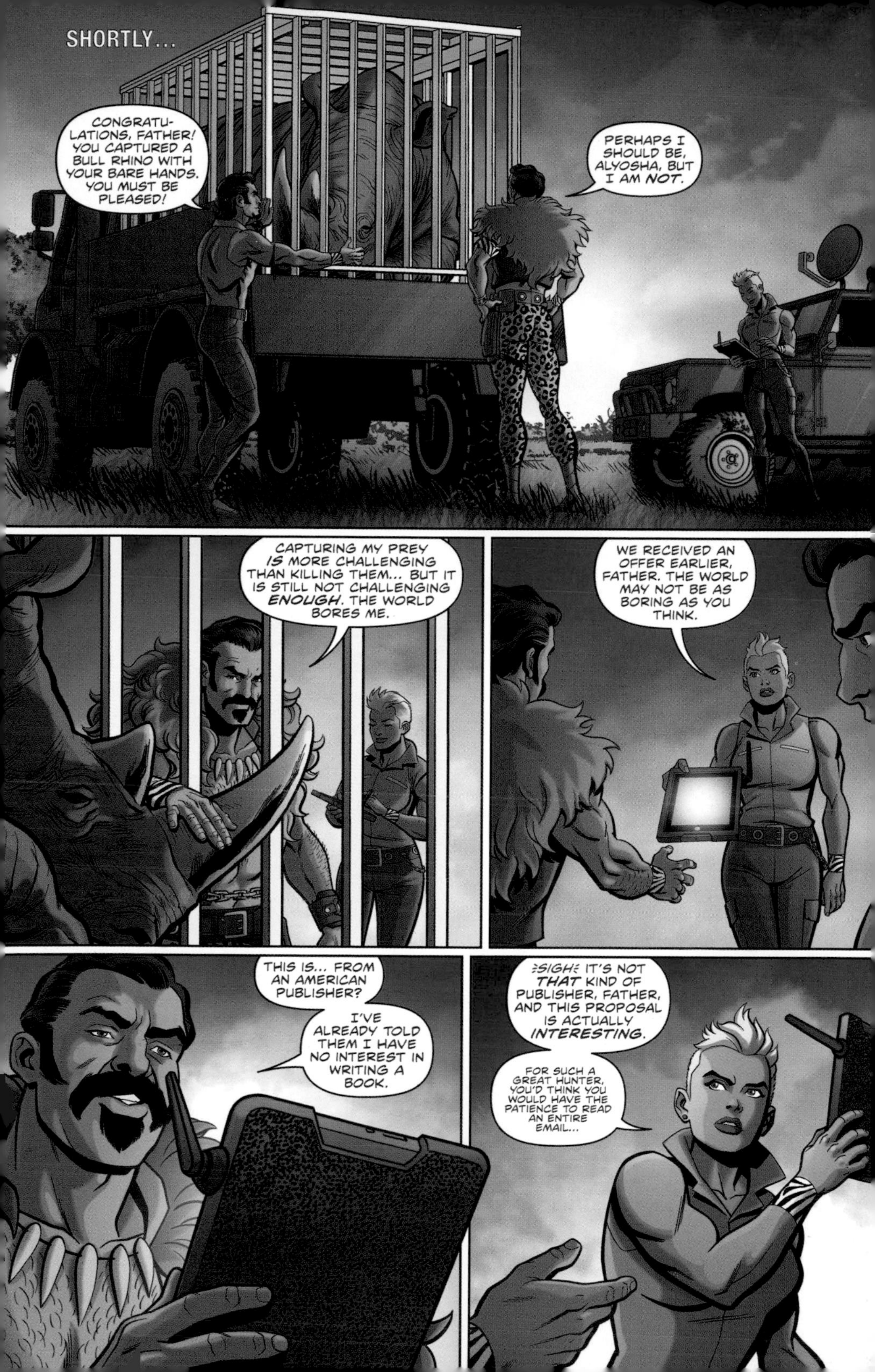
SHORTLY...
CONGRATULATIONS, FATHER! YOU CAPTURED A BULL RHINO WITH YOUR BARE HANDS. YOU MUST BE PLEASED!
PERHAPS I SHOULD BE, ALYOSHA, BUT I AM NOT.
CAPTURING MY PREY IS MORE CHALLENGING THAN KILLING THEM... BUT IT IS STILL NOT CHALLENGING ENOUGH. THE WORLD BORES ME.
WE RECEIVED AN OFFER EARLIER, FATHER. THE WORLD MAY NOT BE AS BORING AS YOU THINK.
THIS IS... FROM AN AMERICAN PUBLISHER?
I'VE ALREADY TOLD THEM I HAVE NO INTEREST IN WRITING A BOOK.
SIGH IT'S NOT THAT KIND OF PUBLISHER, FATHER, AND THIS PROPOSAL IS ACTUALLY INTERESTING.
FOR SUCH A GREAT HUNTER, YOU'D THINK YOU WOULD HAVE THE PATIENCE TO READ AN ENTIRE EMAIL...

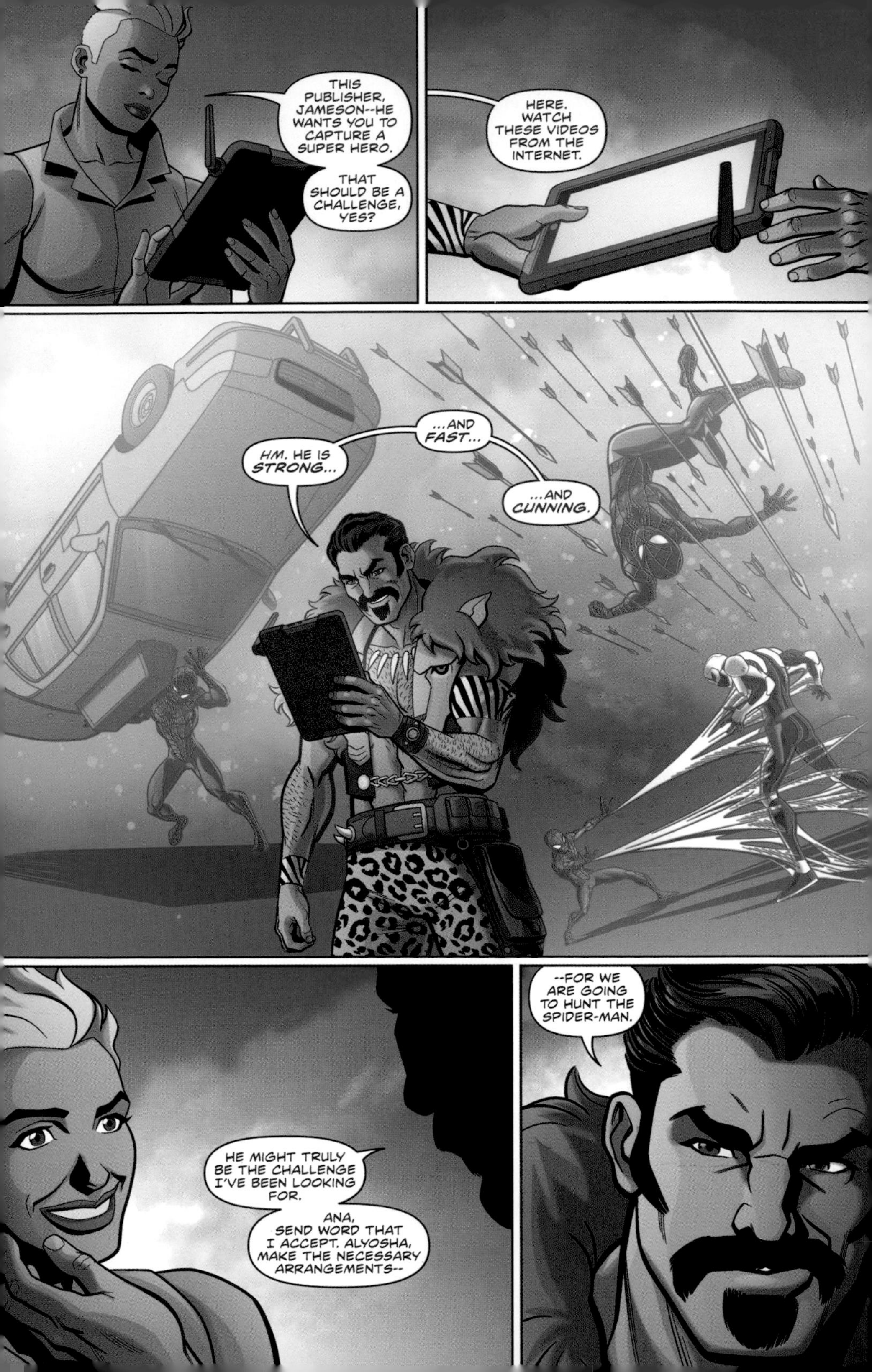
THIS PUBLISHER, JAMESON--HE WANTS YOU TO CAPTURE A SUPER HERO.
THAT SHOULD BE A CHALLENGE, YES?
HERE. WATCH THESE VIDEOS FROM THE INTERNET.
HM. HE IS STRONG...
...AND FAST...
...AND CUNNING.
HE MIGHT TRULY BE THE CHALLENGE I'VE BEEN LOOKING FOR.
ANA, SEND WORD THAT I ACCEPT. ALYOSHA, MAKE THE NECESSARY ARRANGEMENTS--
--FOR WE ARE GOING TO HUNT THE SPIDER-MAN.

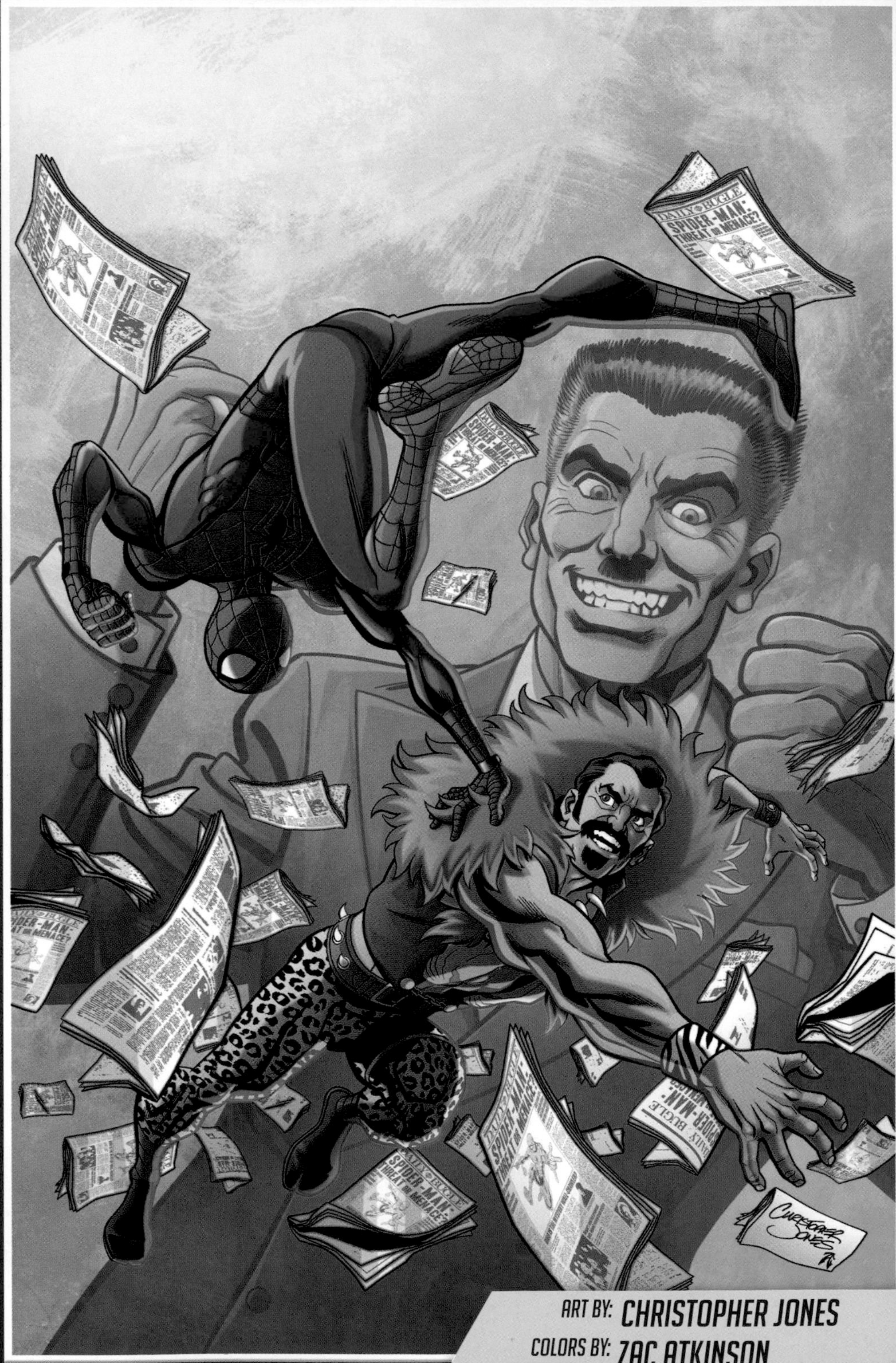
DAILY BUGLE
SPIDER-MAN: THREAT OR MENACE?

ART BY: CHRISTOPHER JONES
COLORS BY: ZAC ATKINSON

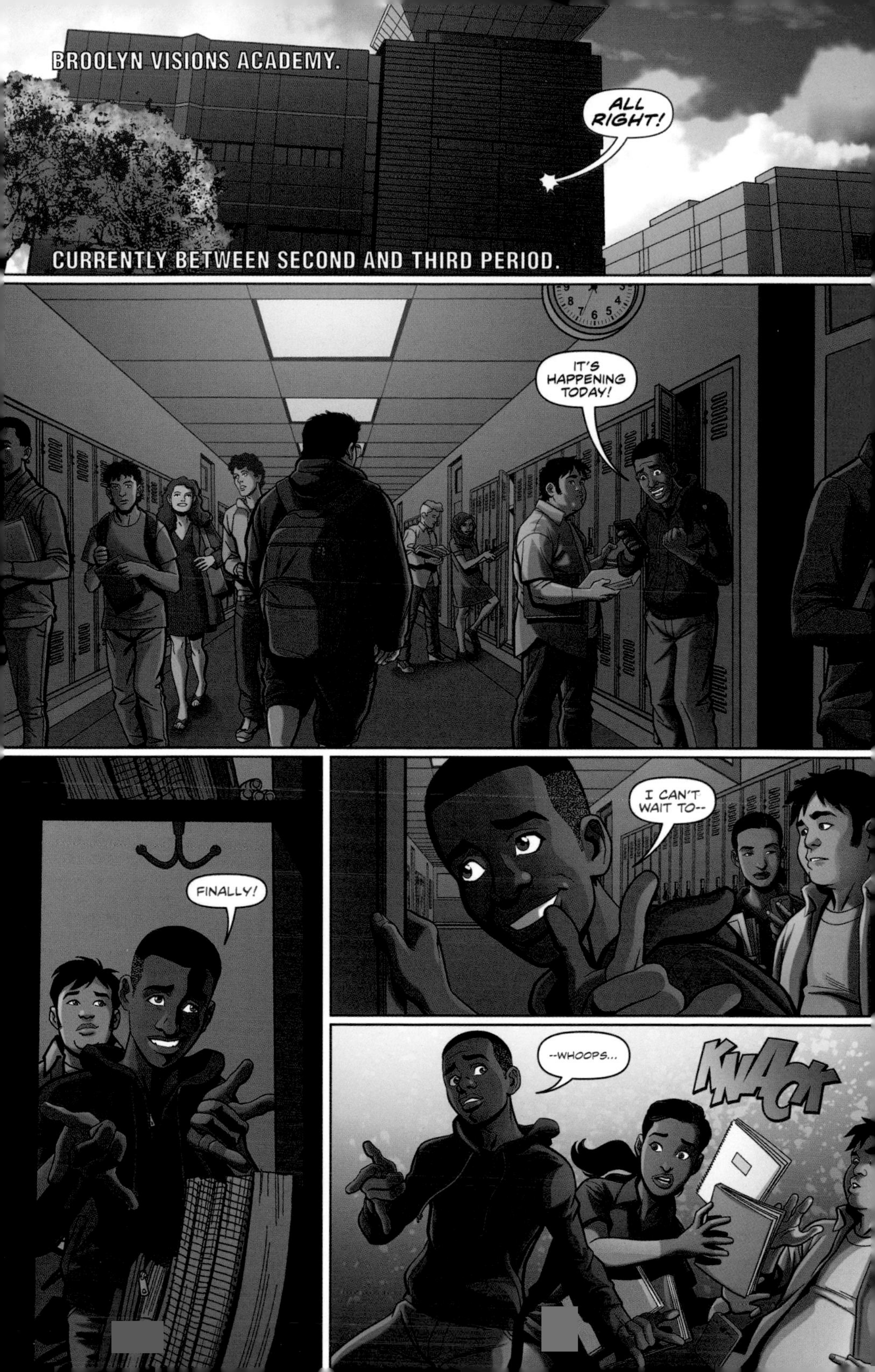
BROOLYN VISIONS ACADEMY.
ALL RIGHT!
CURRENTLY BETWEEN SECOND AND THIRD PERIOD.
IT'S HAPPENING TODAY!
FINALLY!
I CAN'T WAIT TO--
--WHOOPS...

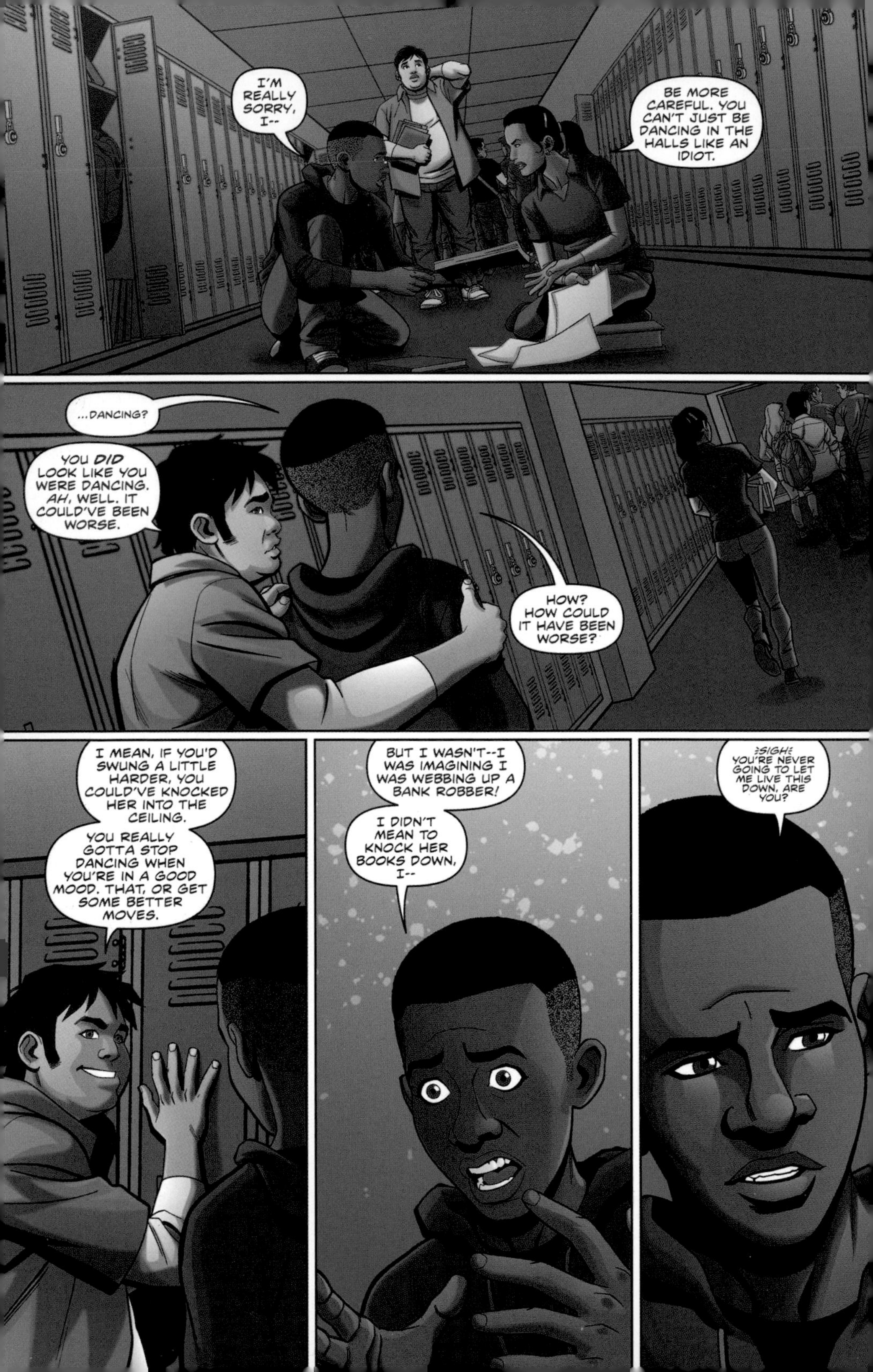
I'M REALLY SORRY, I--
BE MORE CAREFUL. YOU CAN'T JUST BE DANCING IN THE HALLS LIKE AN IDIOT.
...DANCING?
YOU DID LOOK LIKE YOU WERE DANCING. AH, WELL. IT COULD'VE BEEN WORSE.
HOW? HOW COULD IT HAVE BEEN WORSE?
I MEAN, IF YOU'D SWUNG A LITTLE HARDER, YOU COULD'VE KNOCKED HER INTO THE CEILING.
YOU REALLY GOTTA STOP DANCING WHEN YOU'RE IN A GOOD MOOD. THAT, OR GET SOME BETTER MOVES.
BUT I WASN'T--I WAS IMAGINING I WAS WEBBING UP A BANK ROBBER!
I DIDN'T MEAN TO KNOCK HER BOOKS DOWN, I--
SIGH
YOU'RE NEVER GOING TO LET ME LIVE THIS DOWN, ARE YOU?

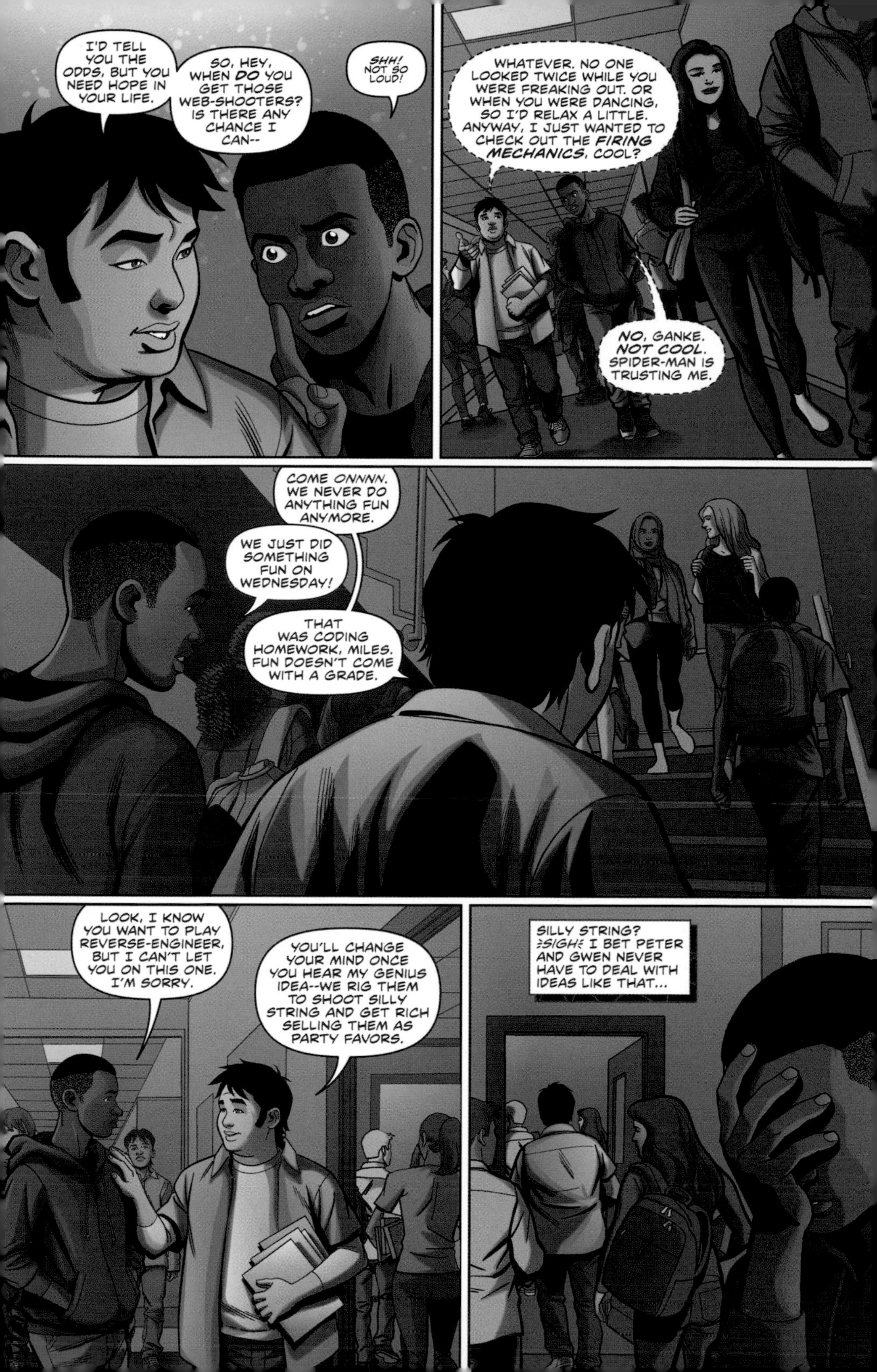
I'D TELL YOU THE ODDS, BUT YOU NEED HOPE IN YOUR LIFE.
SO, HEY, WHEN DO YOU GET THOSE WEB-SHOOTERS? IS THERE ANY CHANCE I CAN--
SHH! NOT SO LOUD!
WHATEVER. NO ONE LOOKED TWICE WHILE YOU WERE FREAKING OUT. OR WHEN YOU WERE DANCING, SO I'D RELAX A LITTLE. ANYWAY, I JUST WANTED TO CHECK OUT THE FIRING MECHANICS, COOL?
NO, GANKE. NOT COOL. SPIDER-MAN IS TRUSTING ME.
COME ONNNN. WE NEVER DO ANYTHING FUN ANYMORE.
WE JUST DID SOMETHING FUN ON WEDNESDAY!
THAT WAS CODING HOMEWORK, MILES. FUN DOESN'T COME WITH A GRADE.
LOOK, I KNOW YOU WANT TO PLAY REVERSE-ENGINEER, BUT I CAN'T LET YOU ON THIS ONE. I'M SORRY.
YOU'LL CHANGE YOUR MIND ONCE YOU HEAR MY GENIUS IDEA--WE RIG THEM TO SHOOT SILLY STRING AND GET RICH SELLING THEM AS PARTY FAVORS.
SILLY STRING? SIGH I BET PETER AND GWEN NEVER HAVE TO DEAL WITH IDEAS LIKE THAT...

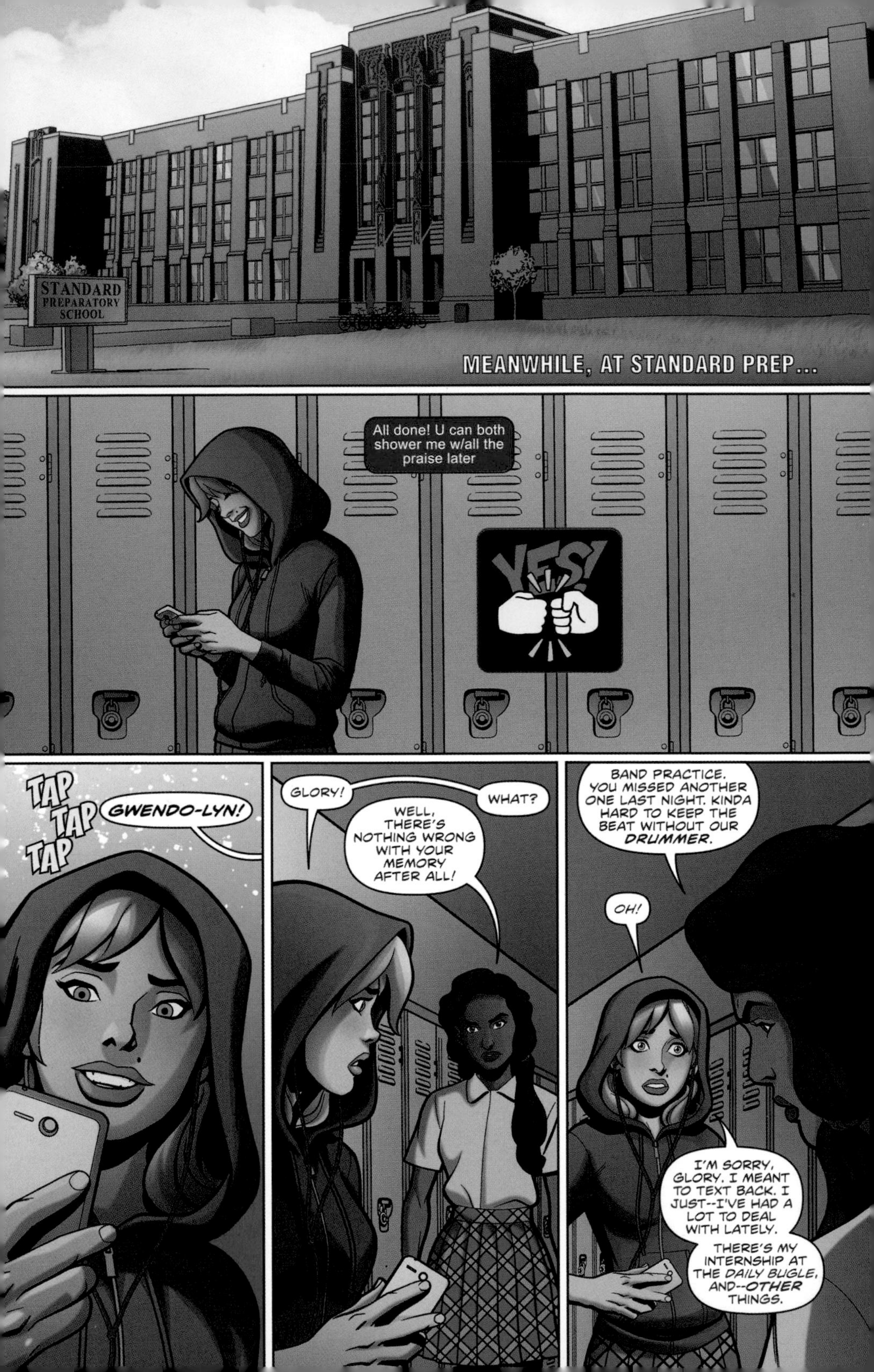
STANDARD PREPARATORY SCHOOL
MEANWHILE, AT STANDARD PREP...
All done! U can both shower me w/all the praise later
YES!
TAP TAP TAP
GWENDO-LYN!
GLORY!
WHAT?
WELL, THERE'S NOTHING WRONG WITH YOUR MEMORY AFTER ALL!
BAND PRACTICE. YOU MISSED ANOTHER ONE LAST NIGHT. KINDA HARD TO KEEP THE BEAT WITHOUT OUR DRUMMER.
OH!
I'M SORRY, GLORY. I MEANT TO TEXT BACK. I JUST--I'VE HAD A LOT TO DEAL WITH LATELY.
THERE'S MY INTERNSHIP AT THE DAILY BUGLE, AND--OTHER THINGS.

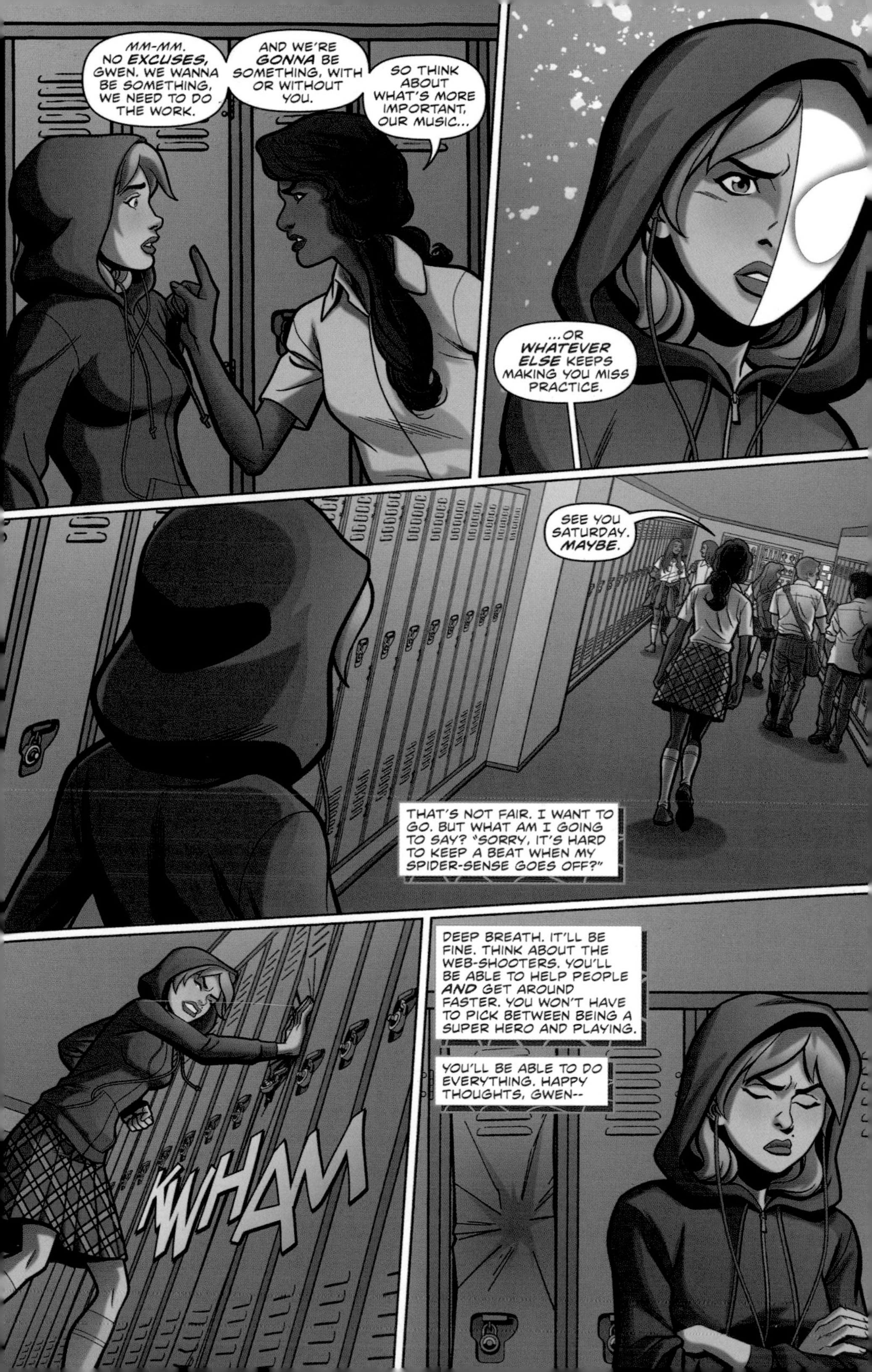
MM-MM. NO EXCUSES, GWEN. WE WANNA BE SOMETHING, WE NEED TO DO THE WORK.
AND WE'RE GONNA BE SOMETHING, WITH OR WITHOUT YOU.
SO THINK ABOUT WHAT'S MORE IMPORTANT, OUR MUSIC...
...OR WHATEVER ELSE KEEPS MAKING YOU MISS PRACTICE.
SEE YOU SATURDAY. MAYBE.
THAT'S NOT FAIR. I WANT TO GO. BUT WHAT AM I GOING TO SAY? "SORRY, IT'S HARD TO KEEP A BEAT WHEN MY SPIDER-SENSE GOES OFF?"
KWHAM
DEEP BREATH. IT'LL BE FINE. THINK ABOUT THE WEB-SHOOTERS. YOU'LL BE ABLE TO HELP PEOPLE AND GET AROUND FASTER. YOU WON'T HAVE TO PICK BETWEEN BEING A SUPER HERO AND PLAYING.
YOU'LL BE ABLE TO DO EVERYTHING. HAPPY THOUGHTS, GWEN--

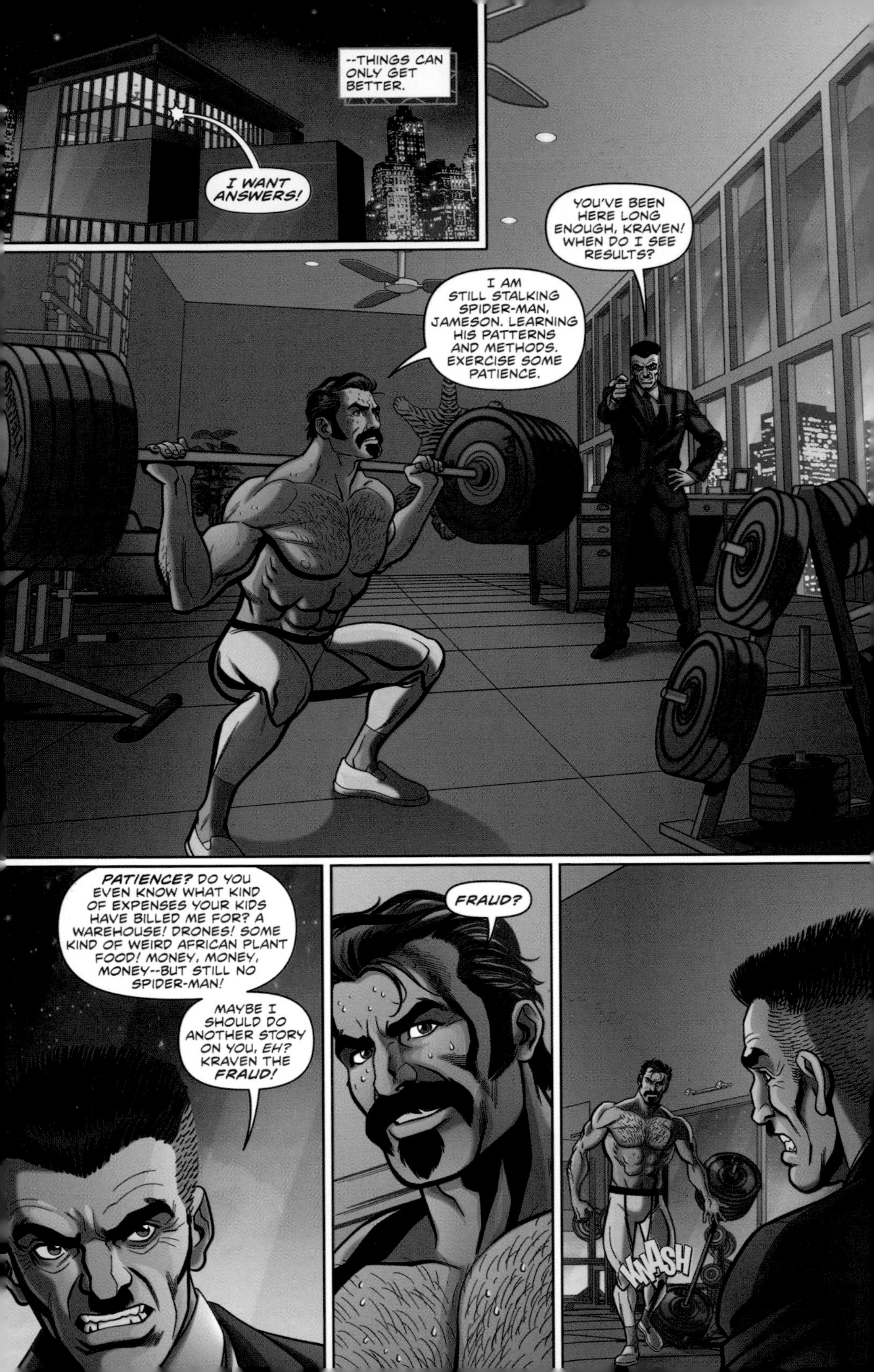
--THINGS CAN ONLY GET BETTER.
I WANT ANSWERS!
YOU'VE BEEN HERE LONG ENOUGH, KRAVEN! WHEN DO I SEE RESULTS?
I AM STILL STALKING SPIDER-MAN, JAMESON. LEARNING HIS PATTERNS AND METHODS. EXERCISE SOME PATIENCE.
PATIENCE? DO YOU EVEN KNOW WHAT KIND OF EXPENSES YOUR KIDS HAVE BILLED ME FOR? A WAREHOUSE! DRONES! SOME KIND OF WEIRD AFRICAN PLANT FOOD! MONEY, MONEY, MONEY--BUT STILL NO SPIDER-MAN!
MAYBE I SHOULD DO ANOTHER STORY ON YOU, EH? KRAVEN THE FRAUD!
FRAUD?
KNASH

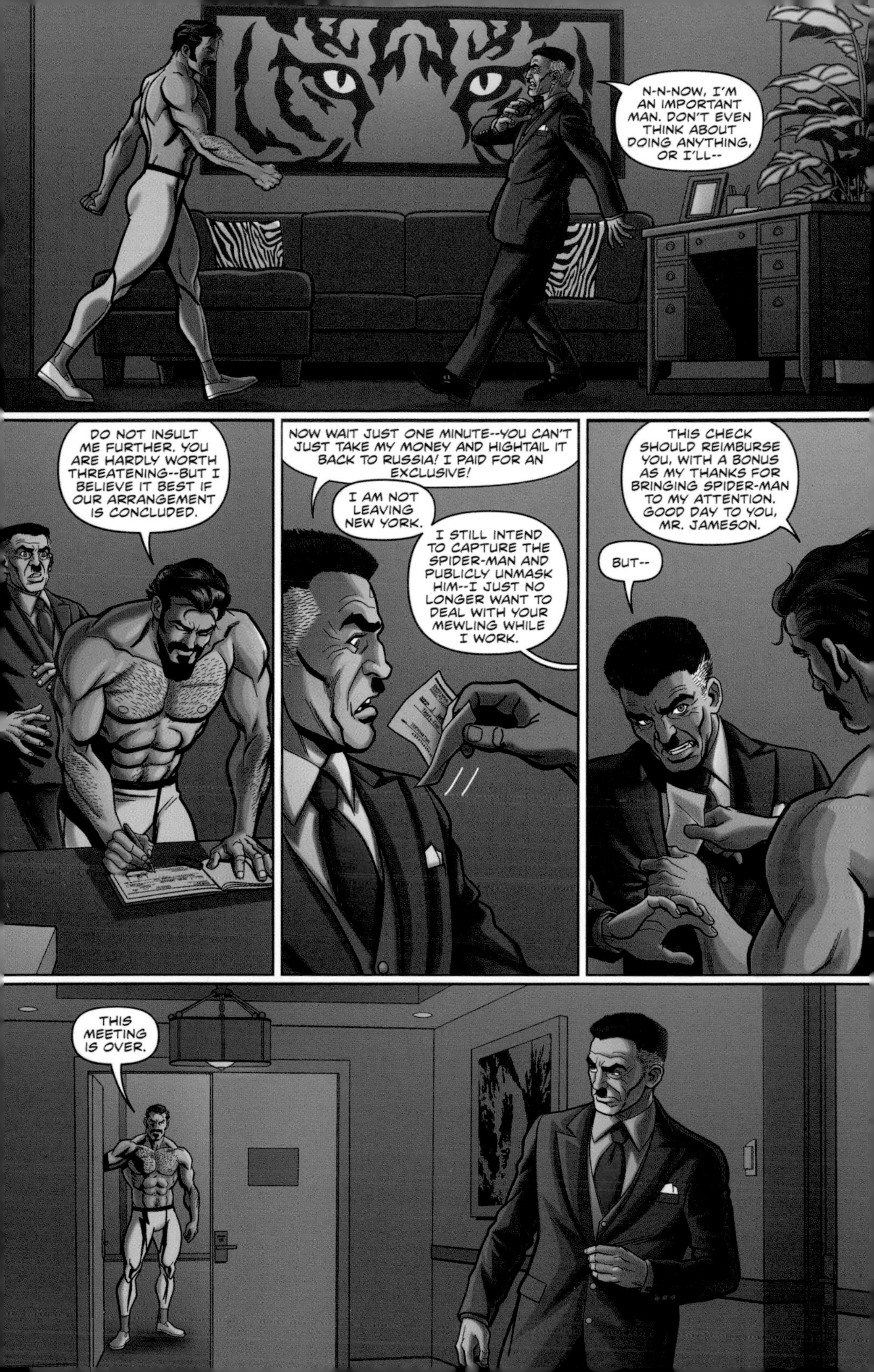
N-N-NOW, I'M AN IMPORTANT MAN. DON'T EVEN THINK ABOUT DOING ANYTHING, OR I'LL--
DO NOT INSULT ME FURTHER. YOU ARE HARDLY WORTH THREATENING--BUT I BELIEVE IT BEST IF OUR ARRANGEMENT IS CONCLUDED.
NOW WAIT JUST ONE MINUTE--YOU CAN'T JUST TAKE MY MONEY AND HIGHTAIL IT BACK TO RUSSIA! I PAID FOR AN EXCLUSIVE!
I AM NOT LEAVING NEW YORK.
I STILL INTEND TO CAPTURE THE SPIDER-MAN AND PUBLICLY UNMASK HIM--I JUST NO LONGER WANT TO DEAL WITH YOUR MEWLING WHILE I WORK.
THIS CHECK SHOULD REIMBURSE YOU, WITH A BONUS AS MY THANKS FOR BRINGING SPIDER-MAN TO MY ATTENTION. GOOD DAY TO YOU, MR. JAMESON.
BUT--
THIS MEETING IS OVER.

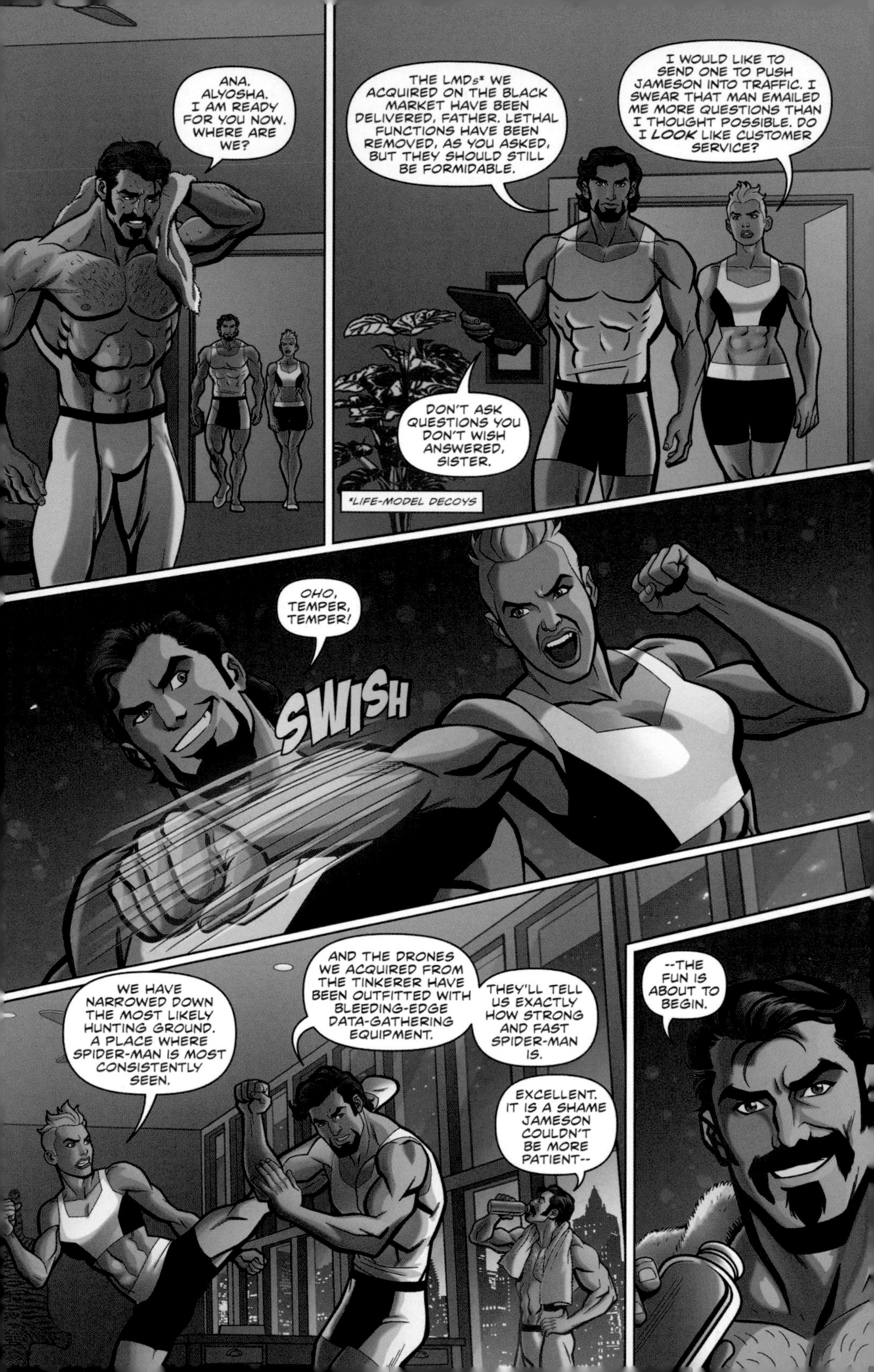
ANA. ALYOSHA. I AM READY FOR YOU NOW. WHERE ARE WE?
THE LMDs* WE ACQUIRED ON THE BLACK MARKET HAVE BEEN DELIVERED, FATHER. LETHAL FUNCTIONS HAVE BEEN REMOVED, AS YOU ASKED, BUT THEY SHOULD STILL BE FORMIDABLE.
I WOULD LIKE TO SEND ONE TO PUSH JAMESON INTO TRAFFIC. I SWEAR THAT MAN EMAILED ME MORE QUESTIONS THAN I THOUGHT POSSIBLE. DO I LOOK LIKE CUSTOMER SERVICE?
DON'T ASK QUESTIONS YOU DON'T WISH ANSWERED, SISTER.
*LIFE-MODEL DECOYS
OHO, TEMPER, TEMPER!
SWISH
WE HAVE NARROWED DOWN THE MOST LIKELY HUNTING GROUND. A PLACE WHERE SPIDER-MAN IS MOST CONSISTENTLY SEEN.
AND THE DRONES WE ACQUIRED FROM THE TINKERER HAVE BEEN OUTFITTED WITH BLEEDING-EDGE DATA-GATHERING EQUIPMENT.
THEY'LL TELL US EXACTLY HOW STRONG AND FAST SPIDER-MAN IS.
EXCELLENT. IT IS A SHAME JAMESON COULDN'T BE MORE PATIENT--
--THE FUN IS ABOUT TO BEGIN.

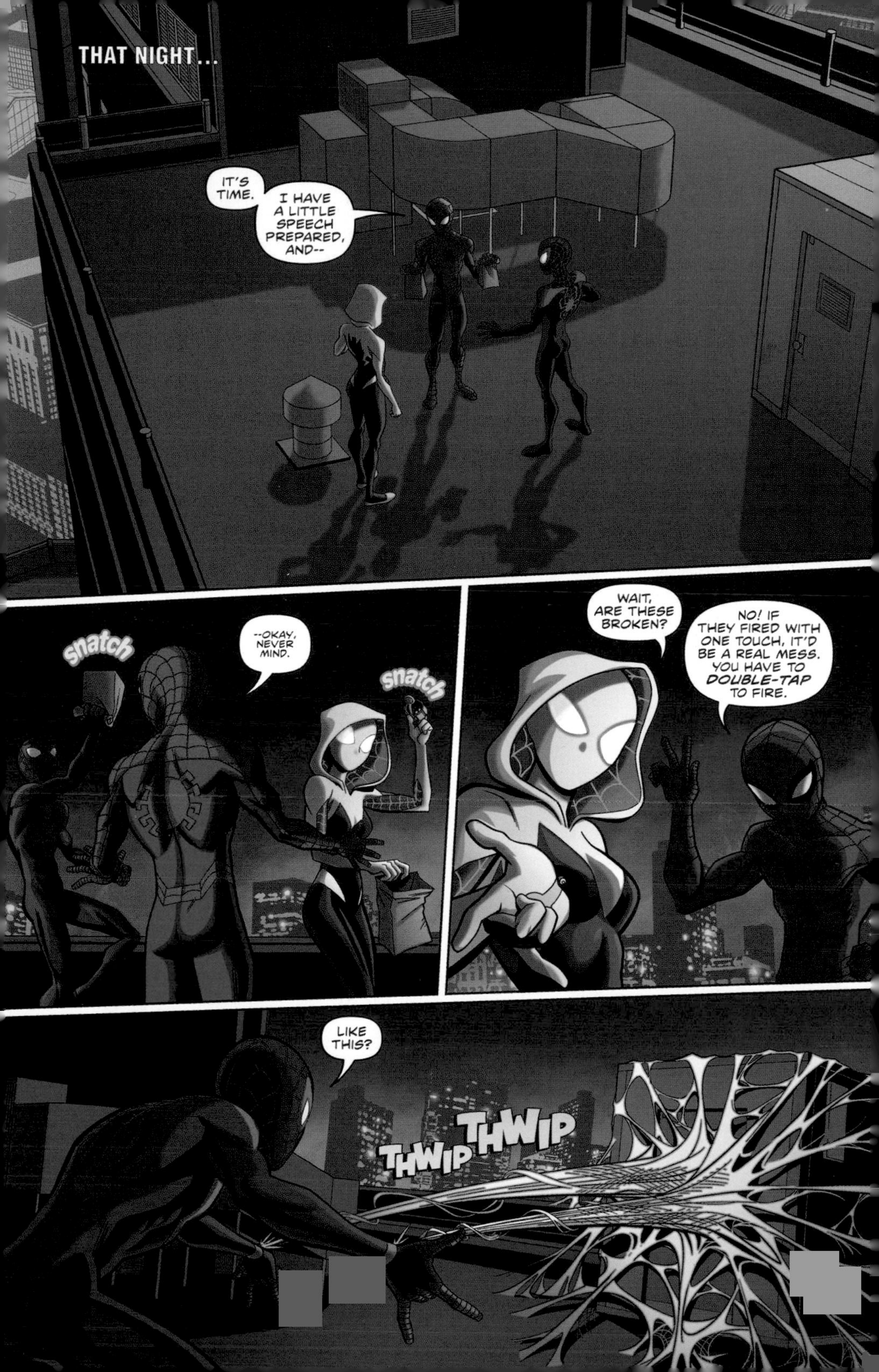
THAT NIGHT...
IT'S TIME.
I HAVE A LITTLE SPEECH PREPARED, AND--
snatch
--OKAY, NEVER MIND.
snatch
WAIT, ARE THESE BROKEN?
NO! IF THEY FIRED WITH ONE TOUCH, IT'D BE A REAL MESS. YOU HAVE TO DOUBLE-TAP TO FIRE.
LIKE THIS?
THWIP THWIP

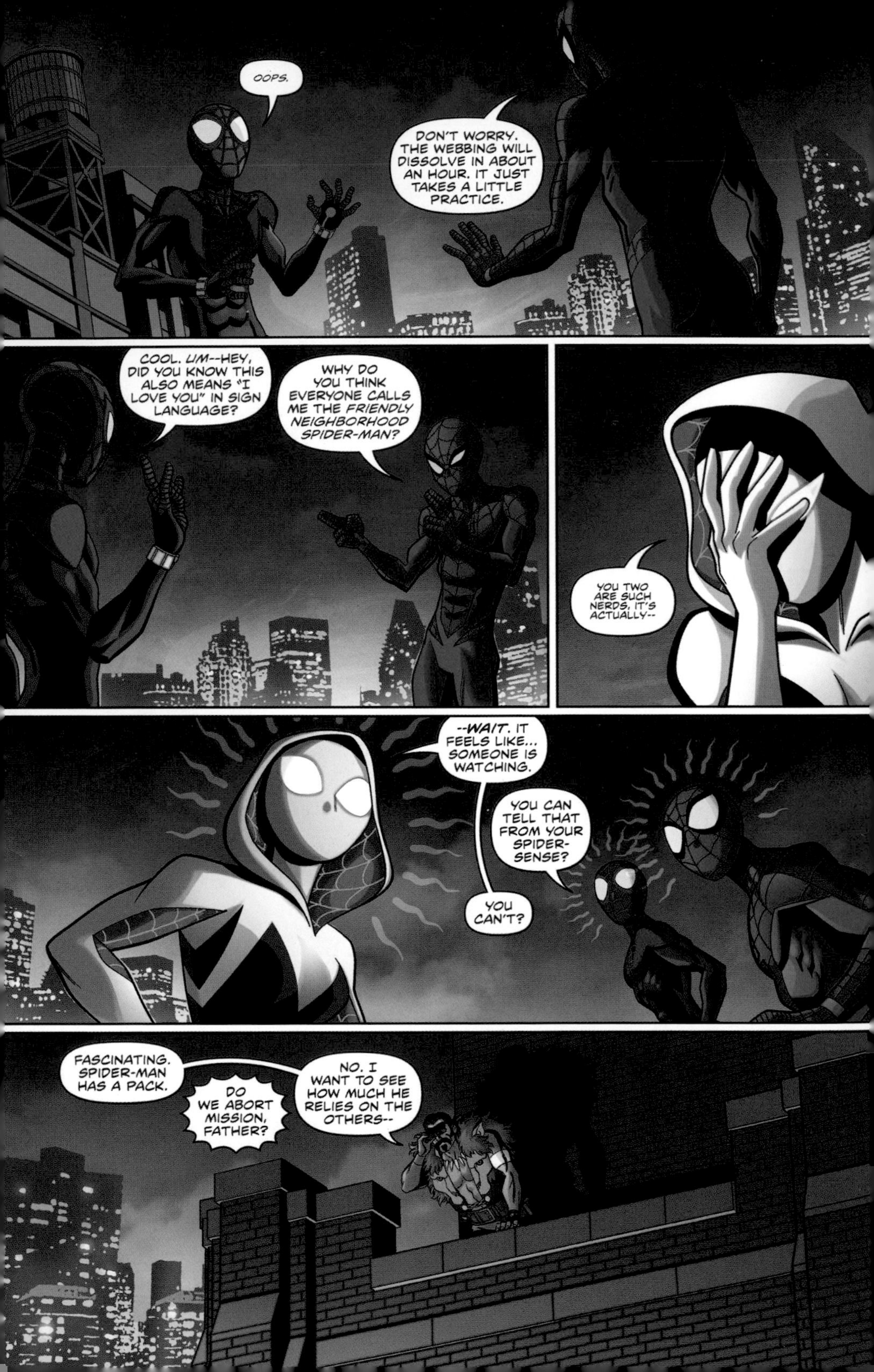
OOPS.
DON'T WORRY. THE WEBBING WILL DISSOLVE IN ABOUT AN HOUR. IT JUST TAKES A LITTLE PRACTICE.
COOL. UM--HEY, DID YOU KNOW THIS ALSO MEANS "I LOVE YOU" IN SIGN LANGUAGE?
WHY DO YOU THINK EVERYONE CALLS ME THE FRIENDLY NEIGHBORHOOD SPIDER-MAN?
YOU TWO ARE SUCH NERDS, IT'S ACTUALLY--
--WAIT. IT FEELS LIKE... SOMEONE IS WATCHING.
YOU CAN TELL THAT FROM YOUR SPIDER-SENSE?
YOU CAN'T?
FASCINATING. SPIDER-MAN HAS A PACK.
DO WE ABORT MISSION, FATHER?
NO. I WANT TO SEE HOW MUCH HE RELIES ON THE OTHERS--

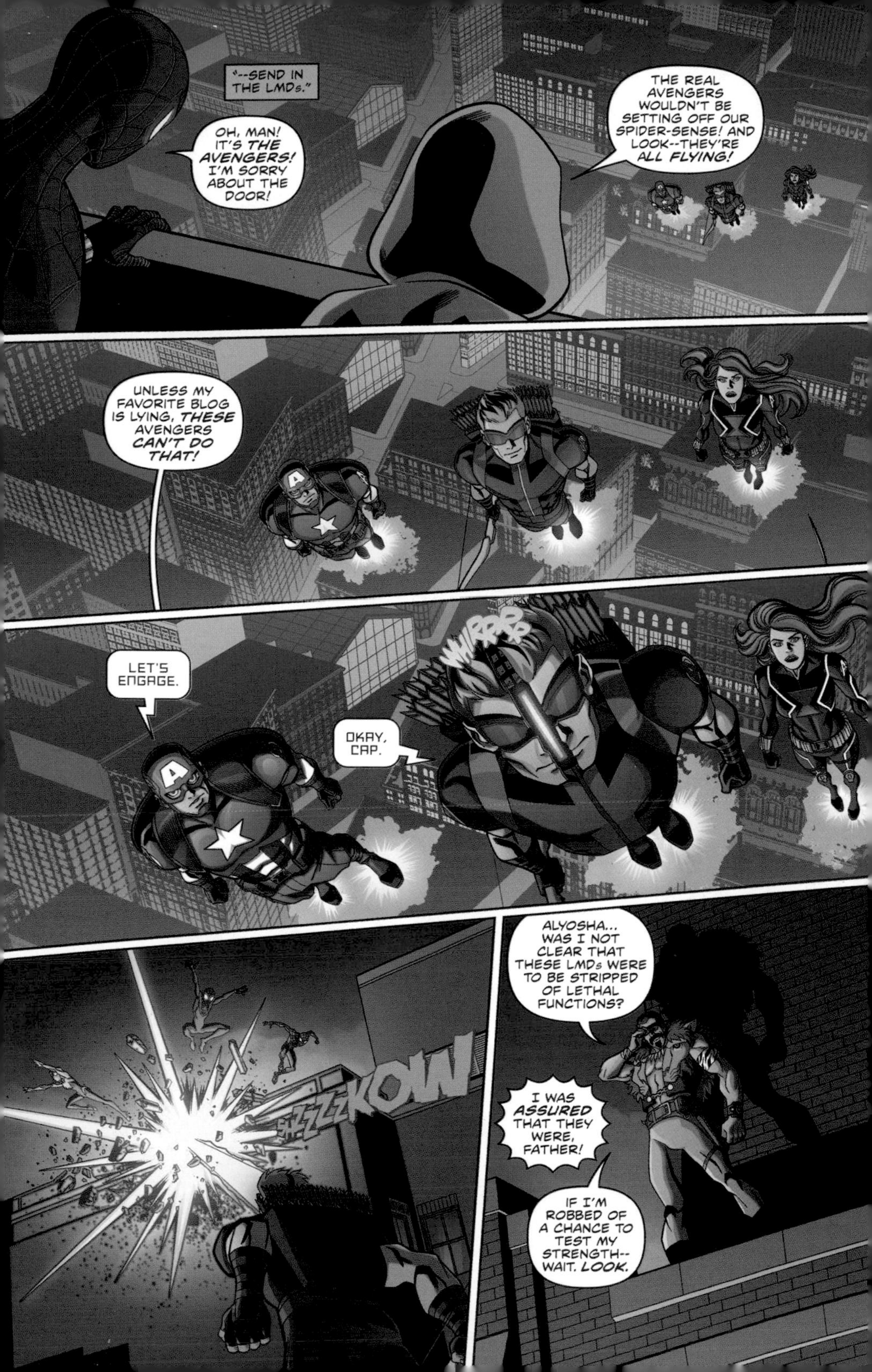
"--SEND IN THE LMDs."
OH, MAN! IT'S THE AVENGERS! I'M SORRY ABOUT THE DOOR!
THE REAL AVENGERS WOULDN'T BE SETTING OFF OUR SPIDER-SENSE! AND LOOK--THEY'RE ALL FLYING!
UNLESS MY FAVORITE BLOG IS LYING, THESE AVENGERS CAN'T DO THAT!
LET'S ENGAGE.
WHIRRRR
OKAY, CAP.
SHZZZ
KOW
ALYOSHA... WAS I NOT CLEAR THAT THESE LMDs WERE TO BE STRIPPED OF LETHAL FUNCTIONS?
I WAS ASSURED THAT THEY WERE, FATHER!
IF I'M ROBBED OF A CHANCE TO TEST MY STRENGTH-- WAIT. LOOK.

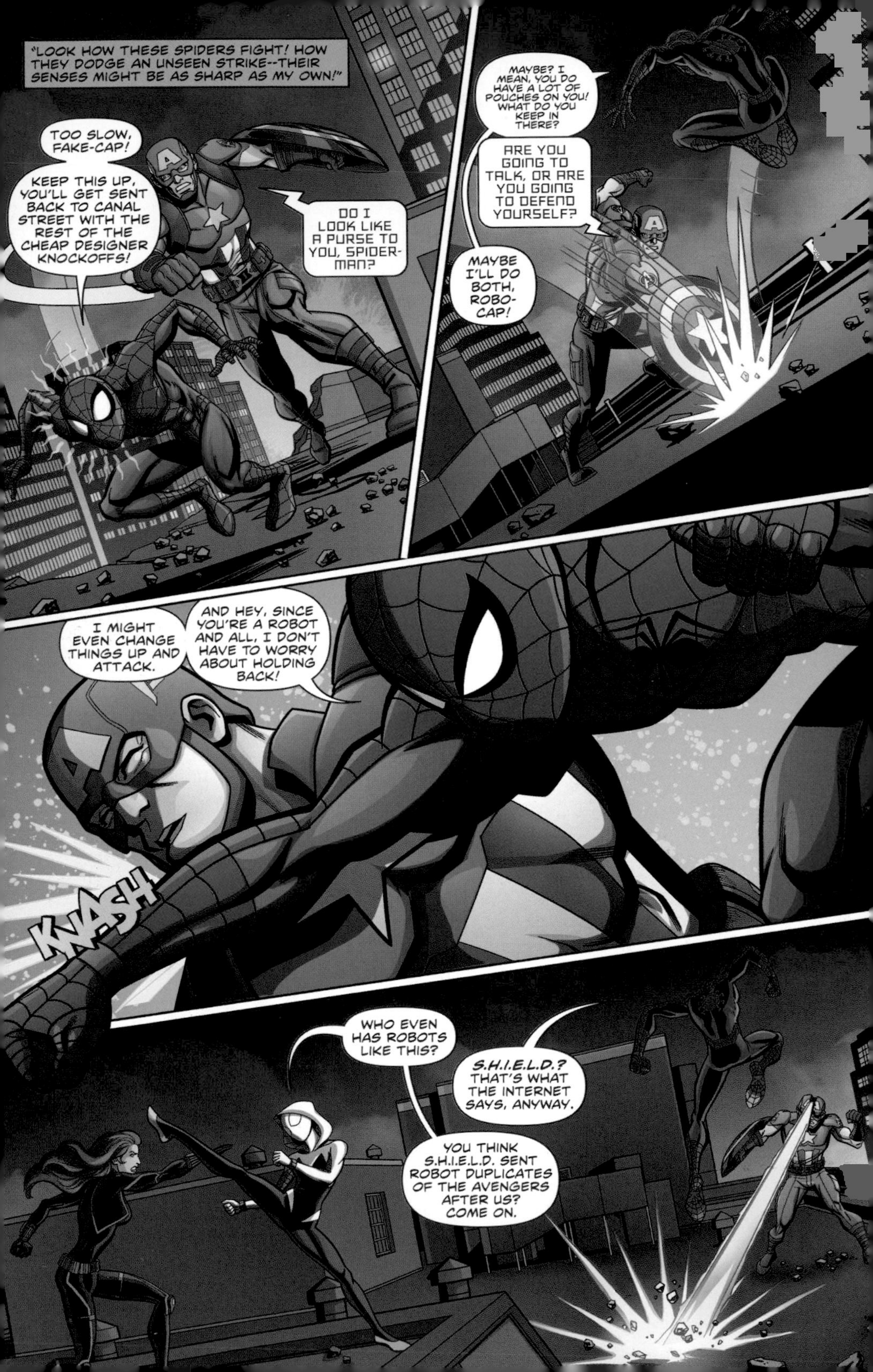
"LOOK HOW THESE SPIDERS FIGHT! HOW THEY DODGE AN UNSEEN STRIKE--THEIR SENSES MIGHT BE AS SHARP AS MY OWN!"
TOO SLOW, FAKE-CAP!
KEEP THIS UP, YOU'LL GET SENT BACK TO CANAL STREET WITH THE REST OF THE CHEAP DESIGNER KNOCKOFFS!
DO I LOOK LIKE A PURSE TO YOU, SPIDER-MAN?
MAYBE? I MEAN, YOU DO HAVE A LOT OF POUCHES ON YOU! WHAT DO YOU KEEP IN THERE?
ARE YOU GOING TO TALK, OR ARE YOU GOING TO DEFEND YOURSELF?
MAYBE I'LL DO BOTH, ROBO-CAP!
I MIGHT EVEN CHANGE THINGS UP AND ATTACK.
AND HEY, SINCE YOU'RE A ROBOT AND ALL, I DON'T HAVE TO WORRY ABOUT HOLDING BACK!
KNASH
WHO EVEN HAS ROBOTS LIKE THIS?
S.H.I.E.L.D.? THAT'S WHAT THE INTERNET SAYS, ANYWAY.
YOU THINK S.H.I.E.L.D. SENT ROBOT DUPLICATES OF THE AVENGERS AFTER US? COME ON.

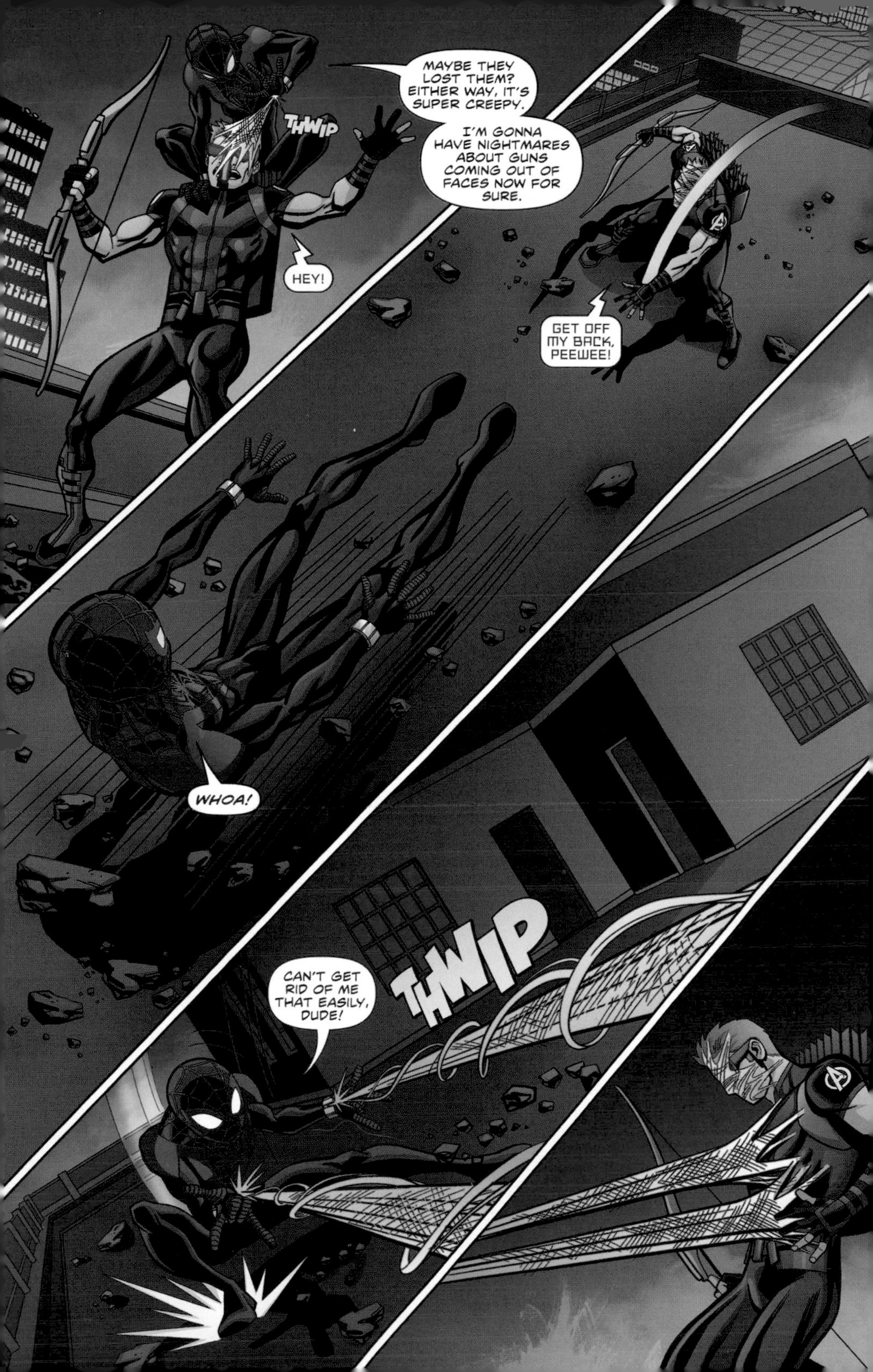
MAYBE THEY LOST THEM? EITHER WAY, IT'S SUPER CREEPY.
I'M GONNA HAVE NIGHTMARES ABOUT GUNS COMING OUT OF FACES NOW FOR SURE.
THWIP
HEY!
GET OFF MY BACK, PEEWEE!
WHOA!
THWIP
CAN'T GET RID OF ME THAT EASILY, DUDE!

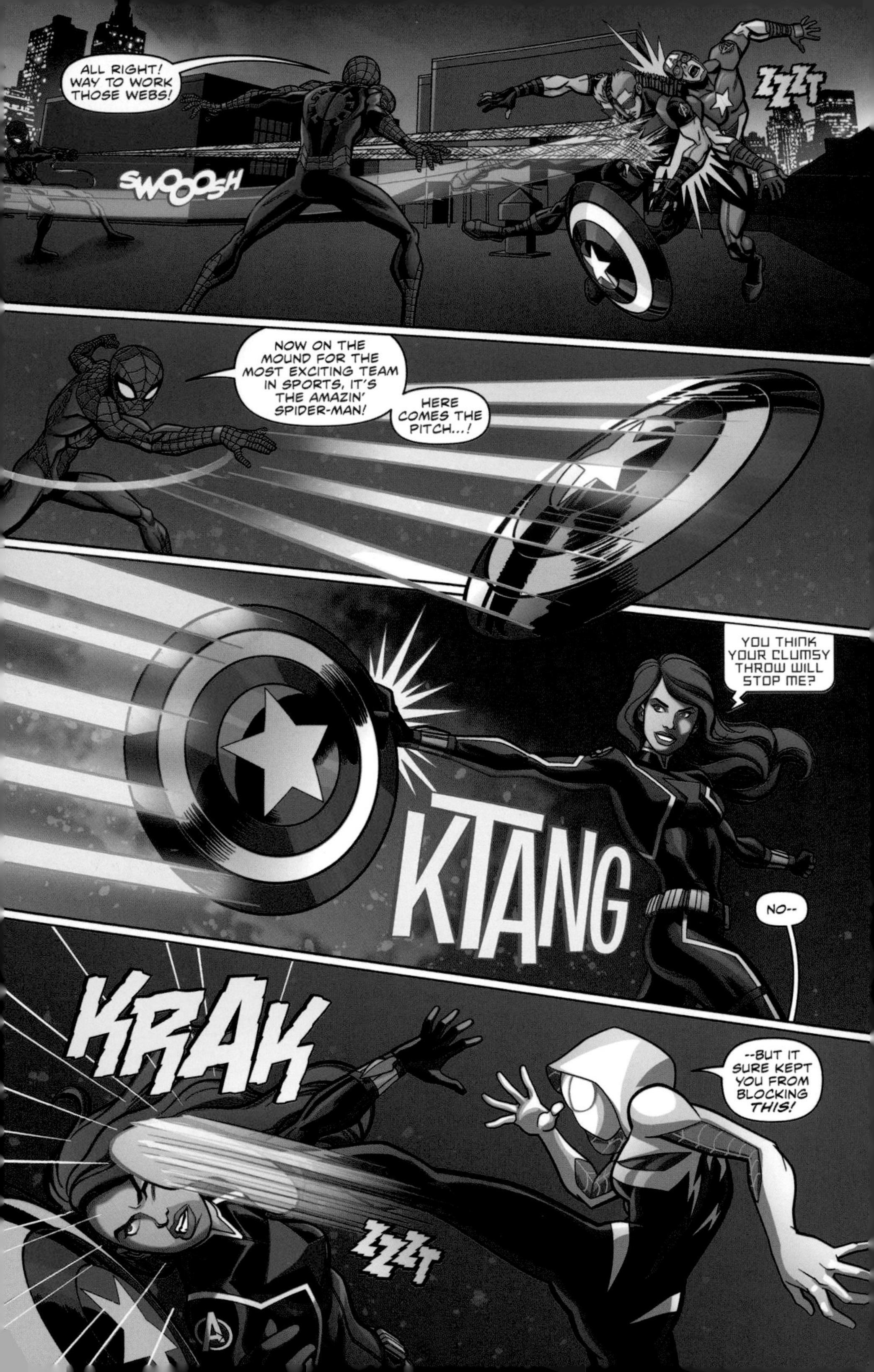
ALL RIGHT! WAY TO WORK THOSE WEBS!
ZZZT
SWOOOSH
NOW ON THE MOUND FOR THE MOST EXCITING TEAM IN SPORTS, IT'S THE AMAZIN' SPIDER-MAN!
HERE COMES THE PITCH...!
YOU THINK YOUR CLUMSY THROW WILL STOP ME?
KTANG
NO--
KRAK
--BUT IT SURE KEPT YOU FROM BLOCKING THIS!
ZZZT

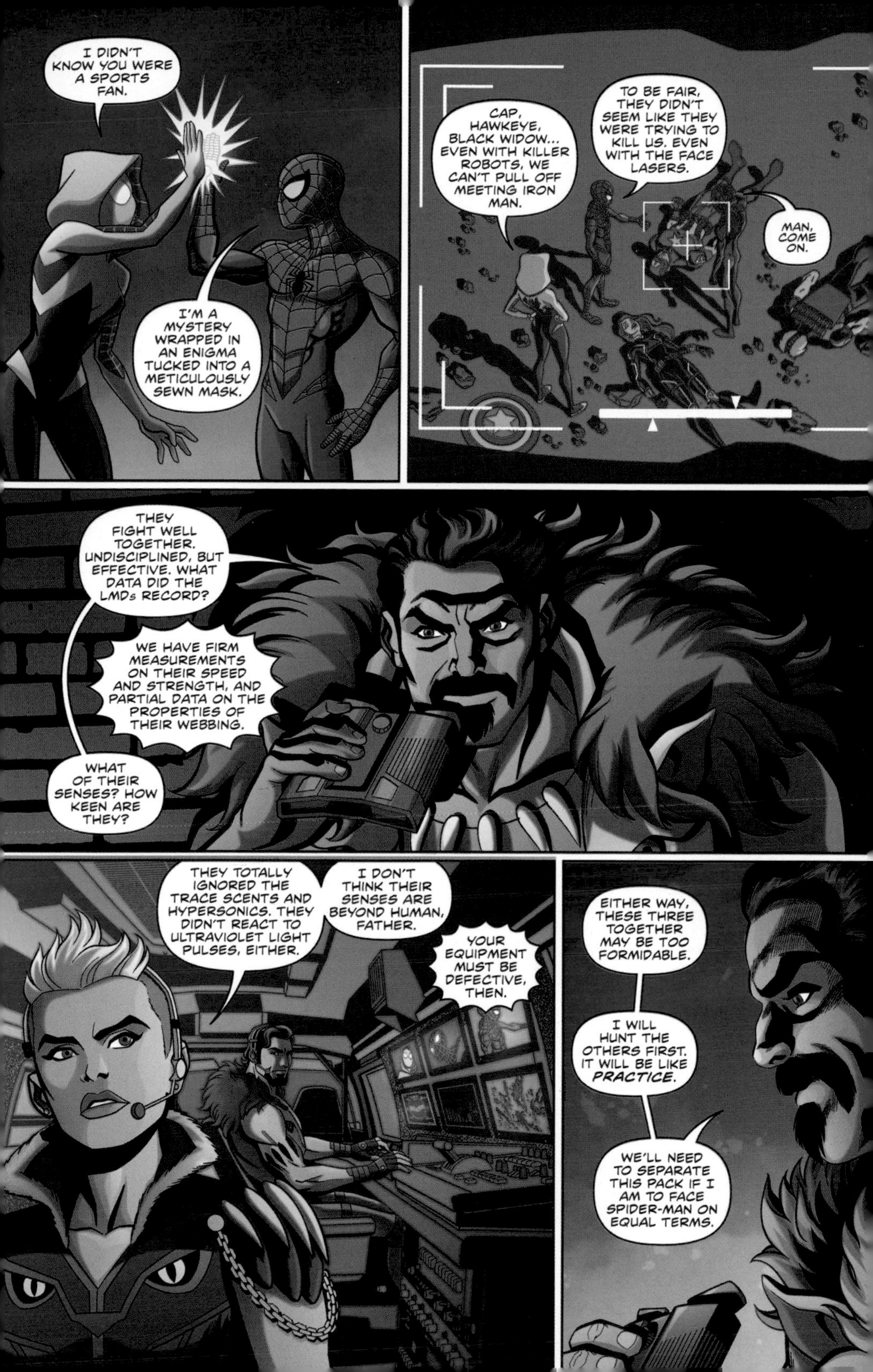
I DIDN'T KNOW YOU WERE A SPORTS FAN.
I'M A MYSTERY WRAPPED IN AN ENIGMA TUCKED INTO A METICULOUSLY SEWN MASK.
CAP, HAWKEYE, BLACK WIDOW... EVEN WITH KILLER ROBOTS, WE CAN'T PULL OFF MEETING IRON MAN.
TO BE FAIR, THEY DIDN'T SEEM LIKE THEY WERE TRYING TO KILL US. EVEN WITH THE FACE LASERS.
MAN, COME ON.
THEY FIGHT WELL TOGETHER. UNDISCIPLINED, BUT EFFECTIVE. WHAT DATA DID THE LMDs RECORD?
WE HAVE FIRM MEASUREMENTS ON THEIR SPEED AND STRENGTH, AND PARTIAL DATA ON THE PROPERTIES OF THEIR WEBBING.
WHAT OF THEIR SENSES? HOW KEEN ARE THEY?
THEY TOTALLY IGNORED THE TRACE SCENTS AND HYPERSONICS. THEY DIDN'T REACT TO ULTRAVIOLET LIGHT PULSES, EITHER.
I DON'T THINK THEIR SENSES ARE BEYOND HUMAN, FATHER.
YOUR EQUIPMENT MUST BE DEFECTIVE, THEN.
EITHER WAY, THESE THREE TOGETHER MAY BE TOO FORMIDABLE.
I WILL HUNT THE OTHERS FIRST. IT WILL BE LIKE *PRACTICE*.
WE'LL NEED TO SEPARATE THIS PACK IF I AM TO FACE SPIDER-MAN ON EQUAL TERMS.

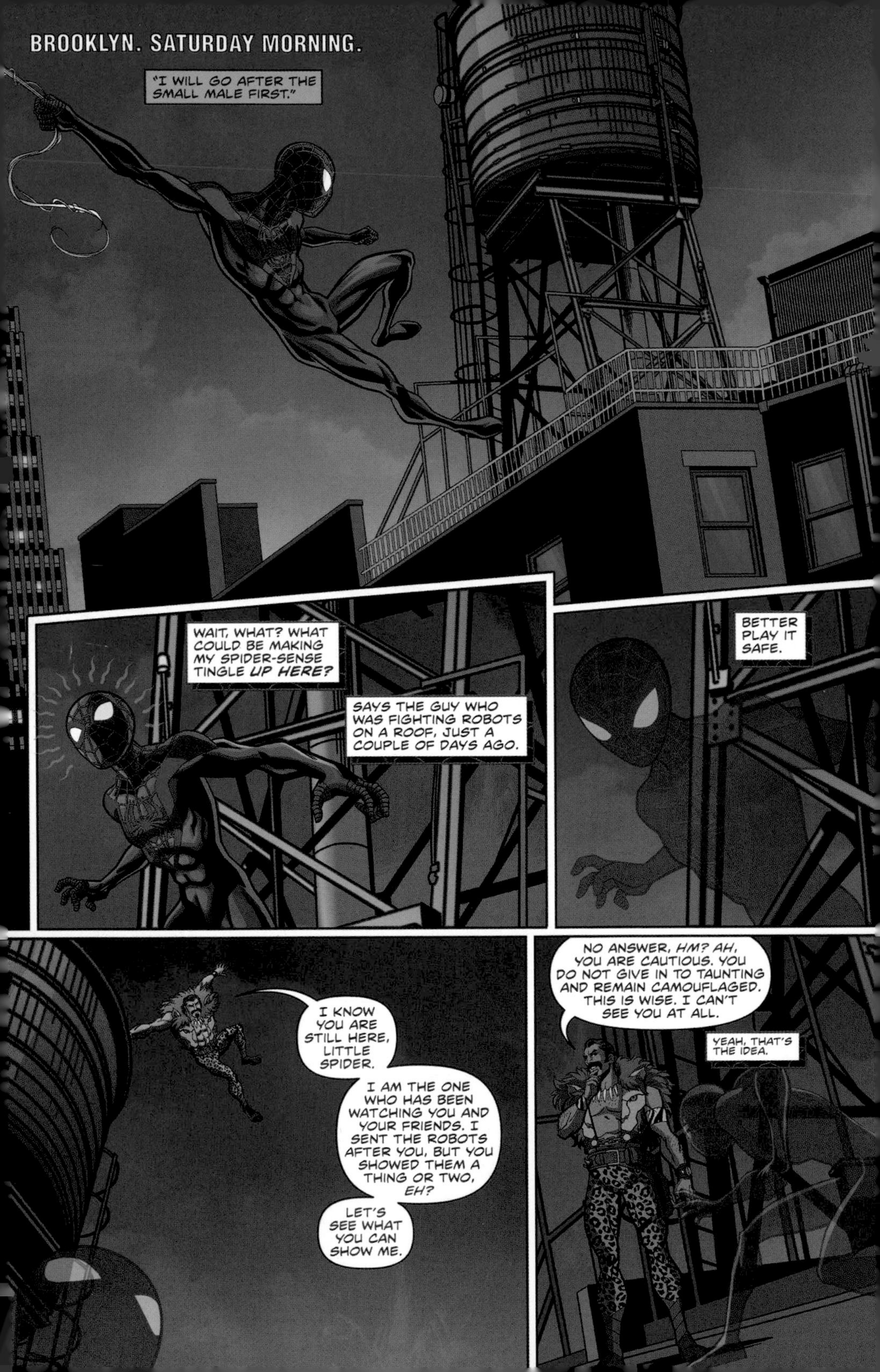
BROOKLYN. SATURDAY MORNING.
"I WILL GO AFTER THE SMALL MALE FIRST."
WAIT, WHAT? WHAT COULD BE MAKING MY SPIDER-SENSE TINGLE UP HERE?
SAYS THE GUY WHO WAS FIGHTING ROBOTS ON A ROOF, JUST A COUPLE OF DAYS AGO.
BETTER PLAY IT SAFE.
I KNOW YOU ARE STILL HERE, LITTLE SPIDER.
I AM THE ONE WHO HAS BEEN WATCHING YOU AND YOUR FRIENDS. I SENT THE ROBOTS AFTER YOU, BUT YOU SHOWED THEM A THING OR TWO, EH?
LET'S SEE WHAT YOU CAN SHOW ME.
NO ANSWER, HM? AH, YOU ARE CAUTIOUS. YOU DO NOT GIVE IN TO TAUNTING AND REMAIN CAMOUFLAGED. THIS IS WISE. I CAN'T SEE YOU AT ALL.
YEAH, THAT'S THE IDEA.

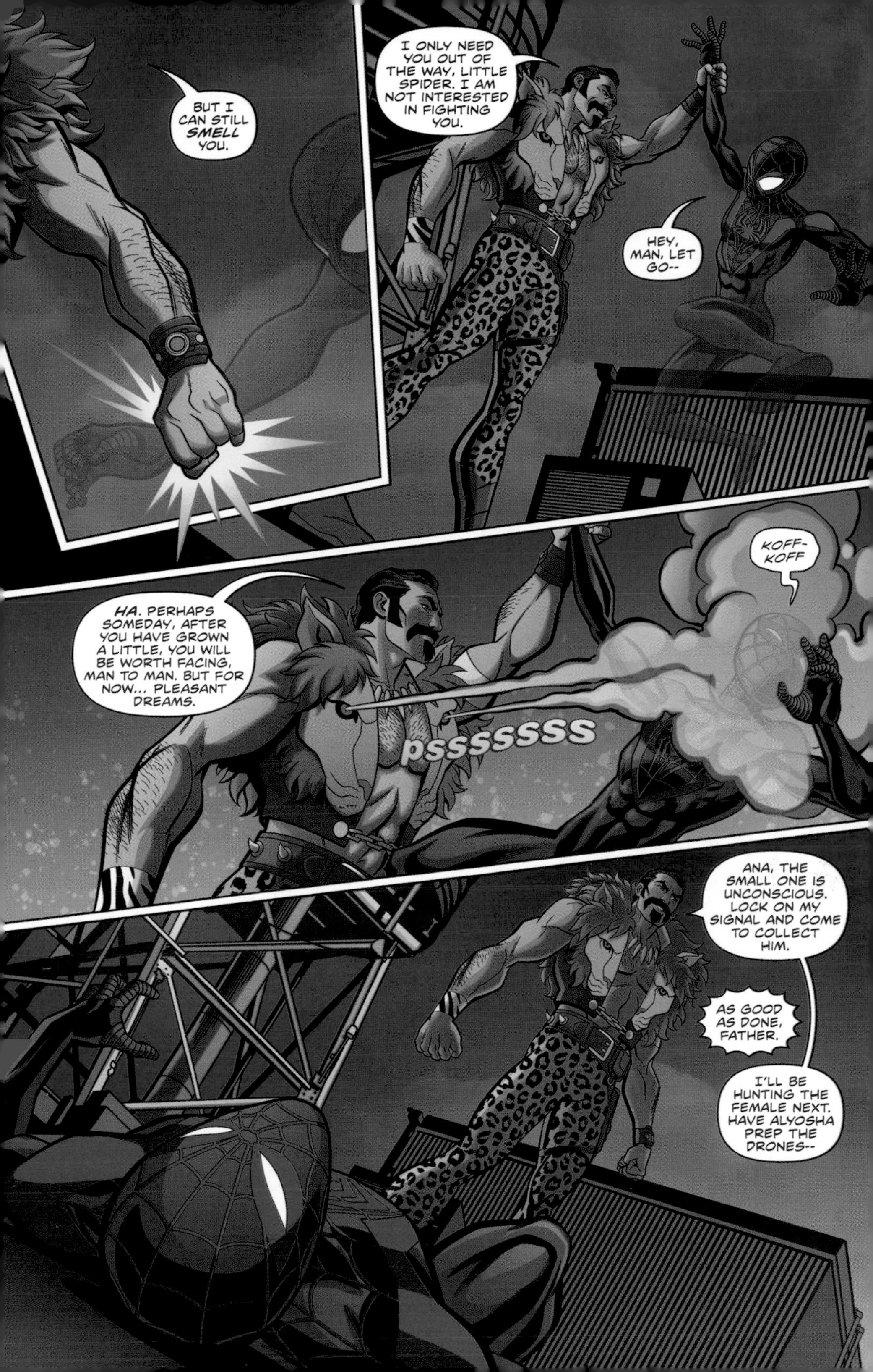
BUT I CAN STILL SMELL YOU.
I ONLY NEED YOU OUT OF THE WAY, LITTLE SPIDER. I AM NOT INTERESTED IN FIGHTING YOU.
HEY, MAN, LET GO--
HA. PERHAPS SOMEDAY, AFTER YOU HAVE GROWN A LITTLE, YOU WILL BE WORTH FACING, MAN TO MAN. BUT FOR NOW... PLEASANT DREAMS.
KOFF-KOFF
pssssssss
ANA, THE SMALL ONE IS UNCONSCIOUS. LOCK ON MY SIGNAL AND COME TO COLLECT HIM.
AS GOOD AS DONE, FATHER.
I'LL BE HUNTING THE FEMALE NEXT. HAVE ALYOSHA PREP THE DRONES--

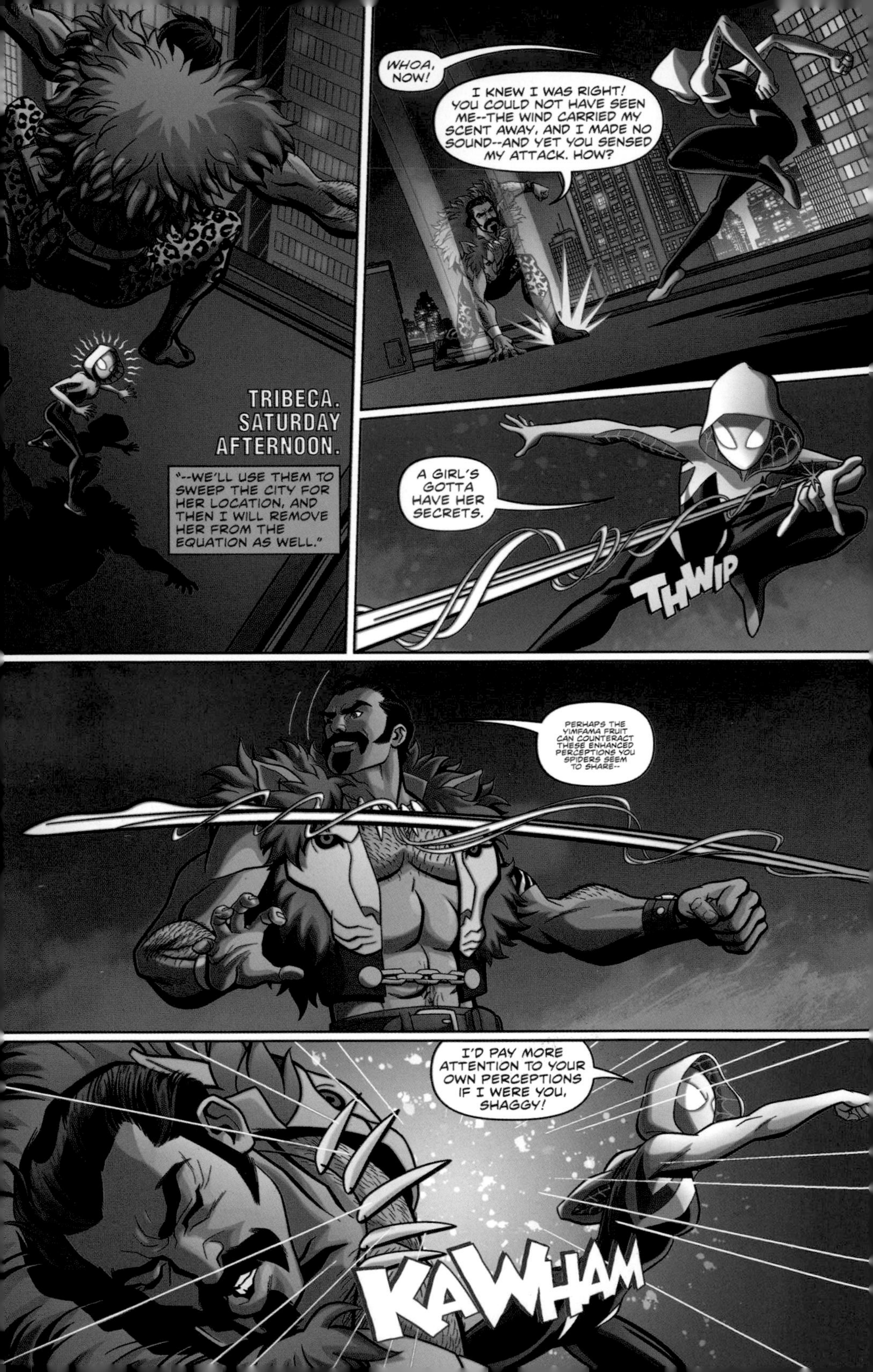
TRIBECA. SATURDAY AFTERNOON.
"--WE'LL USE THEM TO SWEEP THE CITY FOR HER LOCATION, AND THEN I WILL REMOVE HER FROM THE EQUATION AS WELL."
WHOA, NOW!
I KNEW I WAS RIGHT! YOU COULD NOT HAVE SEEN ME--THE WIND CARRIED MY SCENT AWAY, AND I MADE NO SOUND--AND YET YOU SENSED MY ATTACK. HOW?
A GIRL'S GOTTA HAVE HER SECRETS.
THWIP
PERHAPS THE YIMFAMA FRUIT CAN COUNTERACT THESE ENHANCED PERCEPTIONS YOU SPIDERS SEEM TO SHARE--
I'D PAY MORE ATTENTION TO YOUR OWN PERCEPTIONS IF I WERE YOU, SHAGGY!
KAWHAM

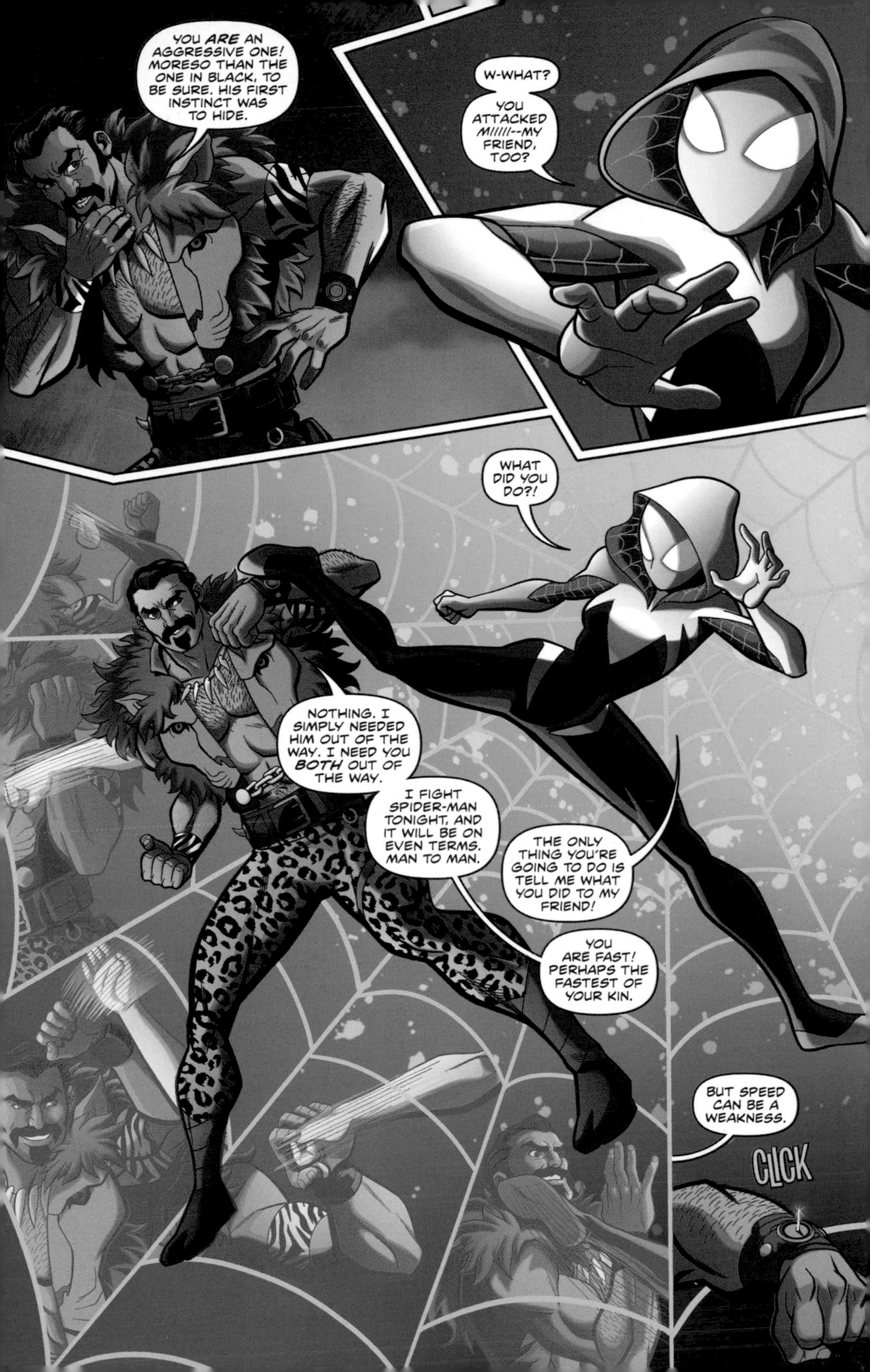
YOU ARE AN AGGRESSIVE ONE! MORESO THAN THE ONE IN BLACK, TO BE SURE. HIS FIRST INSTINCT WAS TO HIDE.
W-WHAT?
YOU ATTACKED M/////--MY FRIEND, TOO?
WHAT DID YOU DO?!
NOTHING. I SIMPLY NEEDED HIM OUT OF THE WAY. I NEED YOU BOTH OUT OF THE WAY.
I FIGHT SPIDER-MAN TONIGHT, AND IT WILL BE ON EVEN TERMS. MAN TO MAN.
THE ONLY THING YOU'RE GOING TO DO IS TELL ME WHAT YOU DID TO MY FRIEND!
YOU ARE FAST! PERHAPS THE FASTEST OF YOUR KIN.
BUT SPEED CAN BE A WEAKNESS.
CLICK

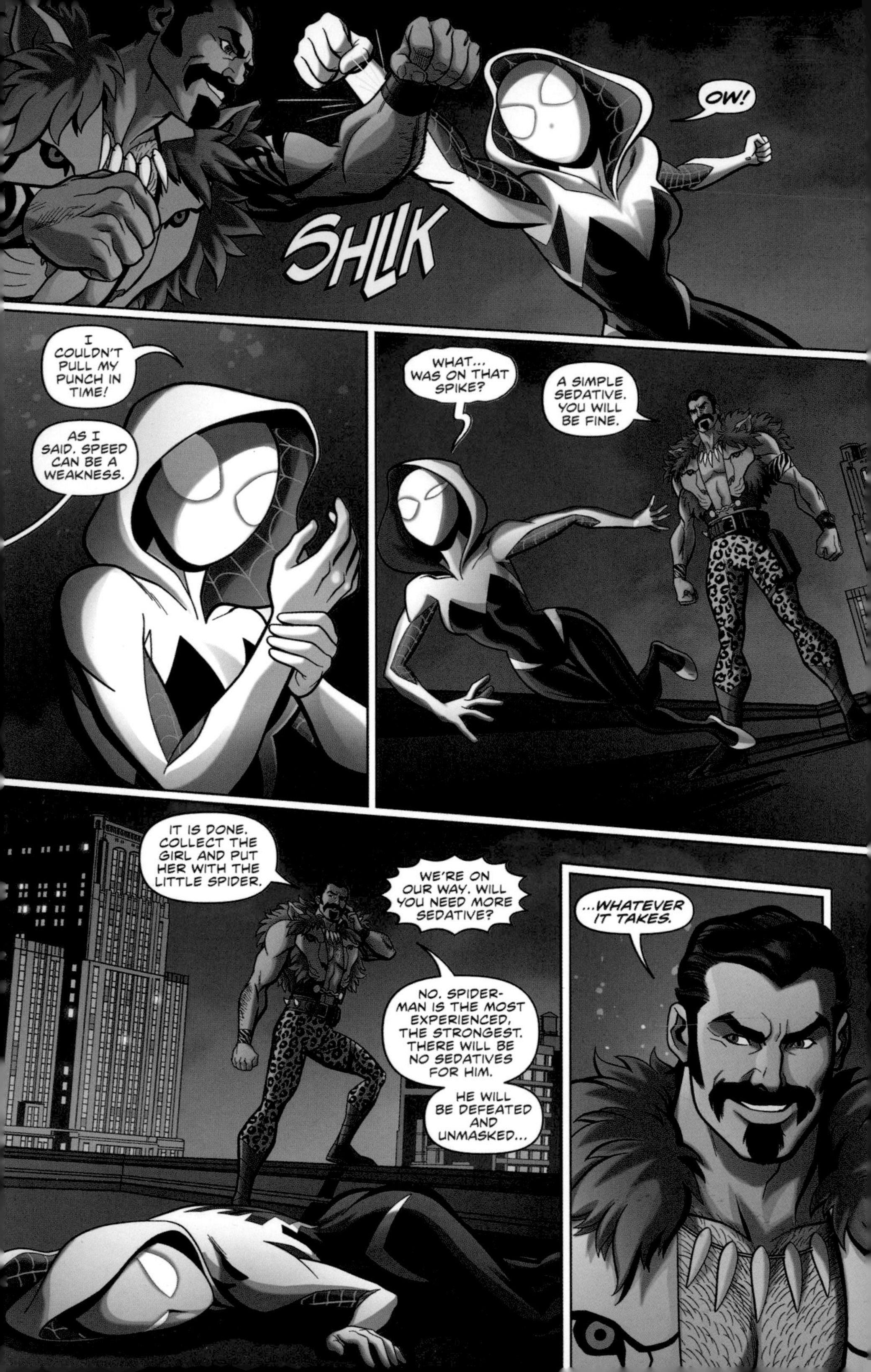
OW!
SHLIK
I COULDN'T PULL MY PUNCH IN TIME!
AS I SAID. SPEED CAN BE A WEAKNESS.
WHAT... WAS ON THAT SPIKE?
A SIMPLE SEDATIVE. YOU WILL BE FINE.
IT IS DONE. COLLECT THE GIRL AND PUT HER WITH THE LITTLE SPIDER.
WE'RE ON OUR WAY. WILL YOU NEED MORE SEDATIVE?
NO. SPIDER-MAN IS THE MOST EXPERIENCED, THE STRONGEST. THERE WILL BE NO SEDATIVES FOR HIM.
HE WILL BE DEFEATED AND UNMASKED...
...WHATEVER IT TAKES.

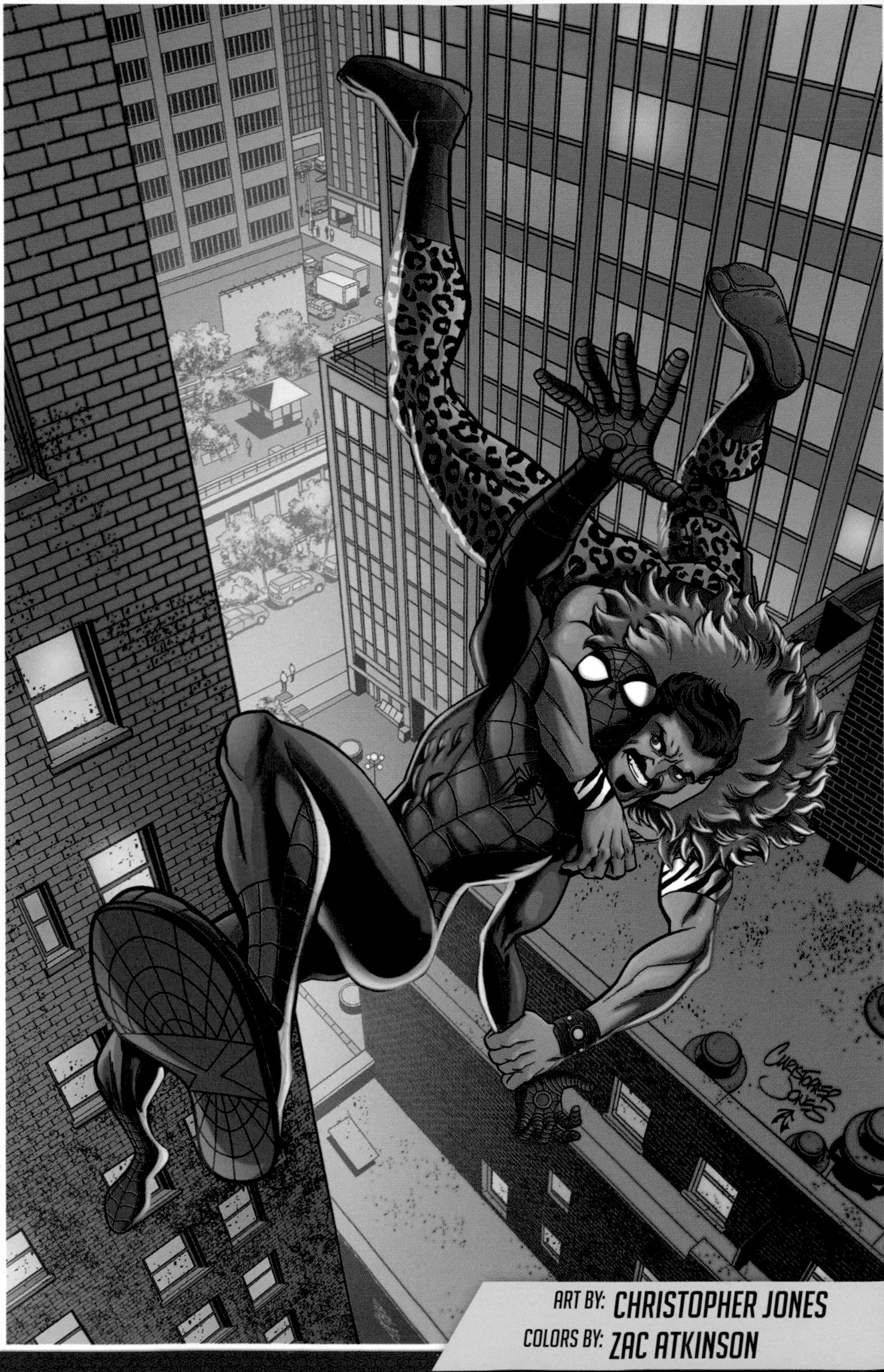
CHRISTOPHER JONES

ART BY: CHRISTOPHER JONES
COLORS BY: ZAC ATKINSON

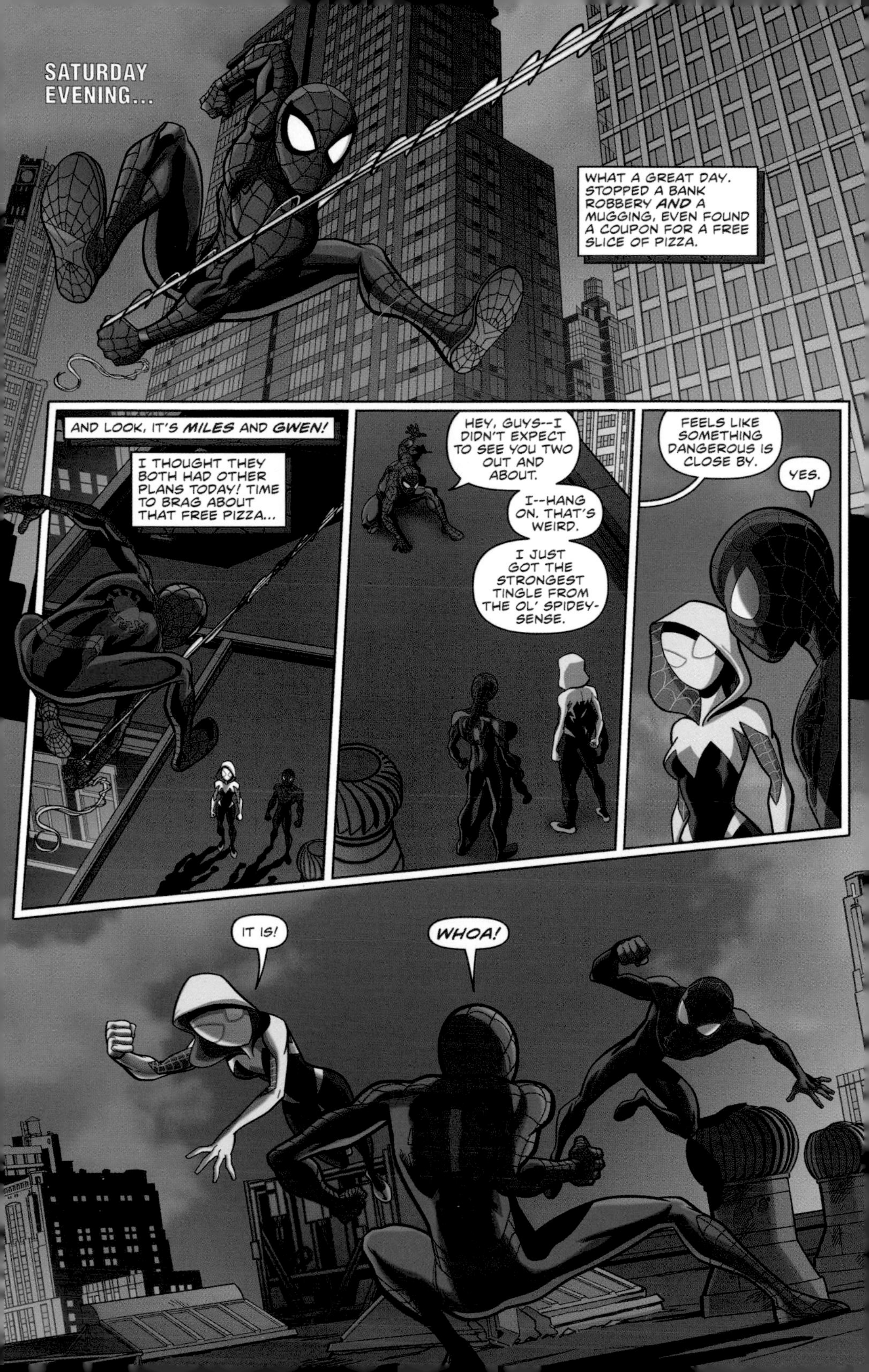

SATURDAY EVENING...
WHAT A GREAT DAY. STOPPED A BANK ROBBERY AND A MUGGING, EVEN FOUND A COUPON FOR A FREE SLICE OF PIZZA.
AND LOOK, IT'S MILES AND GWEN!
I THOUGHT THEY BOTH HAD OTHER PLANS TODAY! TIME TO BRAG ABOUT THAT FREE PIZZA...
HEY, GUYS--I DIDN'T EXPECT TO SEE YOU TWO OUT AND ABOUT.
I--HANG ON. THAT'S WEIRD.
I JUST GOT THE STRONGEST TINGLE FROM THE OL' SPIDEY-SENSE.
FEELS LIKE SOMETHING DANGEROUS IS CLOSE BY.
YES.
IT IS!
WHOA!

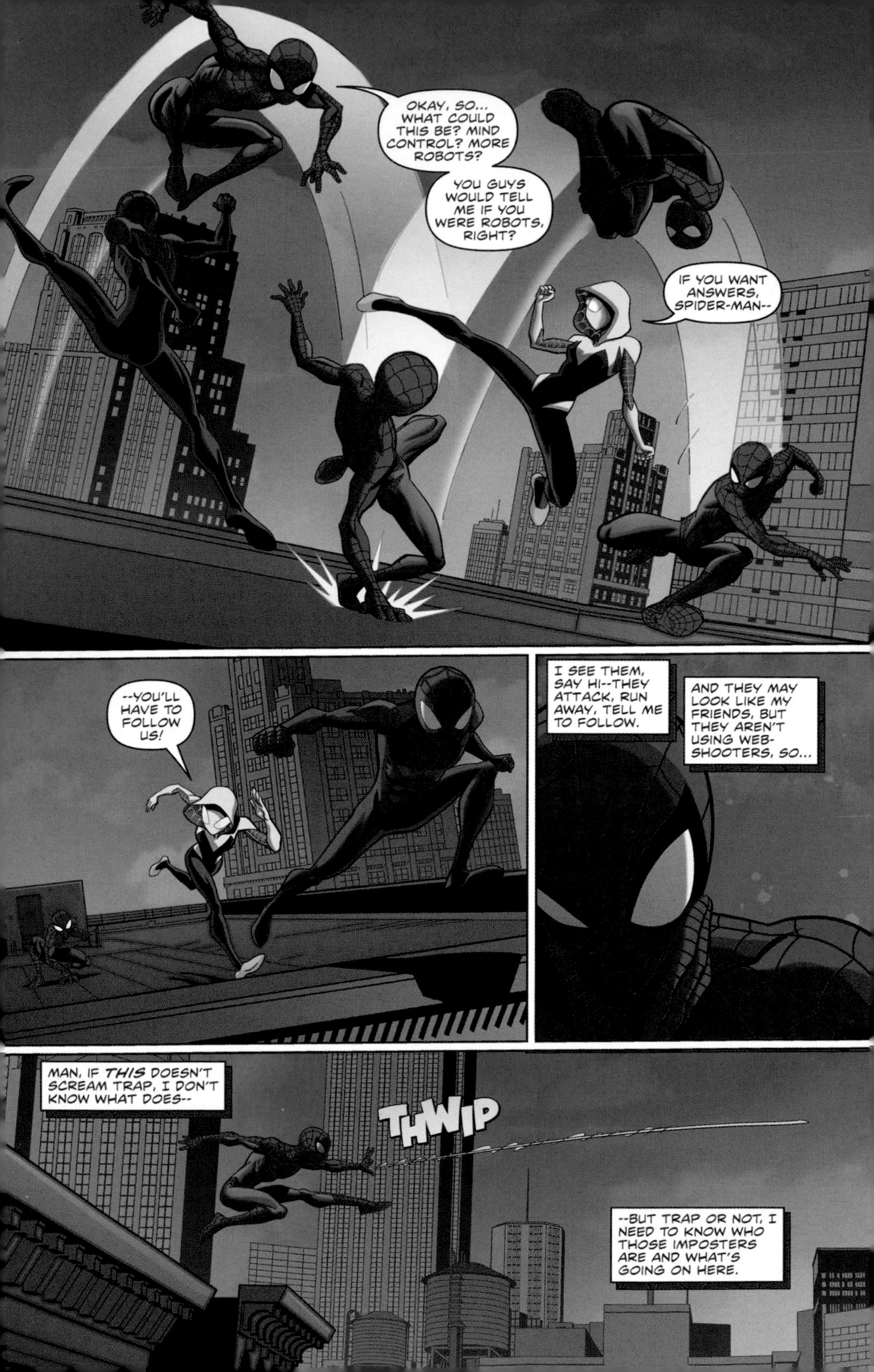
OKAY, SO... WHAT COULD THIS BE? MIND CONTROL? MORE ROBOTS?
YOU GUYS WOULD TELL ME IF YOU WERE ROBOTS, RIGHT?
IF YOU WANT ANSWERS, SPIDER-MAN--
--YOU'LL HAVE TO FOLLOW US!
I SEE THEM, SAY HI--THEY ATTACK, RUN AWAY, TELL ME TO FOLLOW.
AND THEY MAY LOOK LIKE MY FRIENDS, BUT THEY AREN'T USING WEB-SHOOTERS, SO...
MAN, IF THIS DOESN'T SCREAM TRAP, I DON'T KNOW WHAT DOES--
THWIP
--BUT TRAP OR NOT, I NEED TO KNOW WHO THOSE IMPOSTERS ARE AND WHAT'S GOING ON HERE.

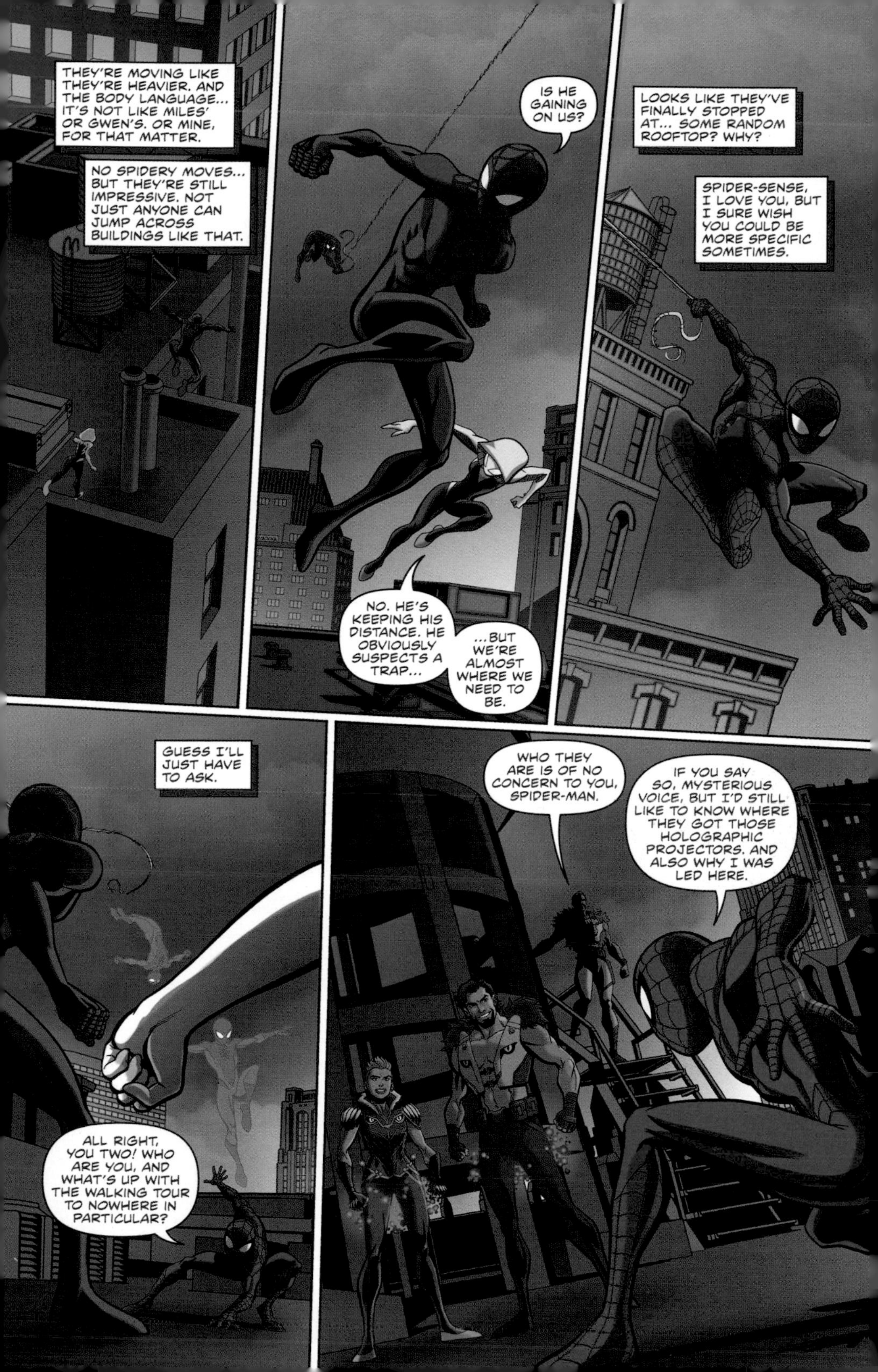

THEY'RE MOVING LIKE THEY'RE HEAVIER. AND THE BODY LANGUAGE... IT'S NOT LIKE MILES' OR GWEN'S. OR MINE, FOR THAT MATTER.
NO SPIDERY MOVES... BUT THEY'RE STILL IMPRESSIVE. NOT JUST ANYONE CAN JUMP ACROSS BUILDINGS LIKE THAT.
IS HE GAINING ON US?
NO. HE'S KEEPING HIS DISTANCE. HE OBVIOUSLY SUSPECTS A TRAP...
...BUT WE'RE ALMOST WHERE WE NEED TO BE.
LOOKS LIKE THEY'VE FINALLY STOPPED AT... SOME RANDOM ROOFTOP? WHY?
SPIDER-SENSE, I LOVE YOU, BUT I SURE WISH YOU COULD BE MORE SPECIFIC SOMETIMES.
GUESS I'LL JUST HAVE TO ASK.
ALL RIGHT, YOU TWO! WHO ARE YOU, AND WHAT'S UP WITH THE WALKING TOUR TO NOWHERE IN PARTICULAR?
WHO THEY ARE IS OF NO CONCERN TO YOU, SPIDER-MAN.
IF YOU SAY SO, MYSTERIOUS VOICE, BUT I'D STILL LIKE TO KNOW WHERE THEY GOT THOSE HOLOGRAPHIC PROJECTORS. AND ALSO WHY I WAS LED HERE.

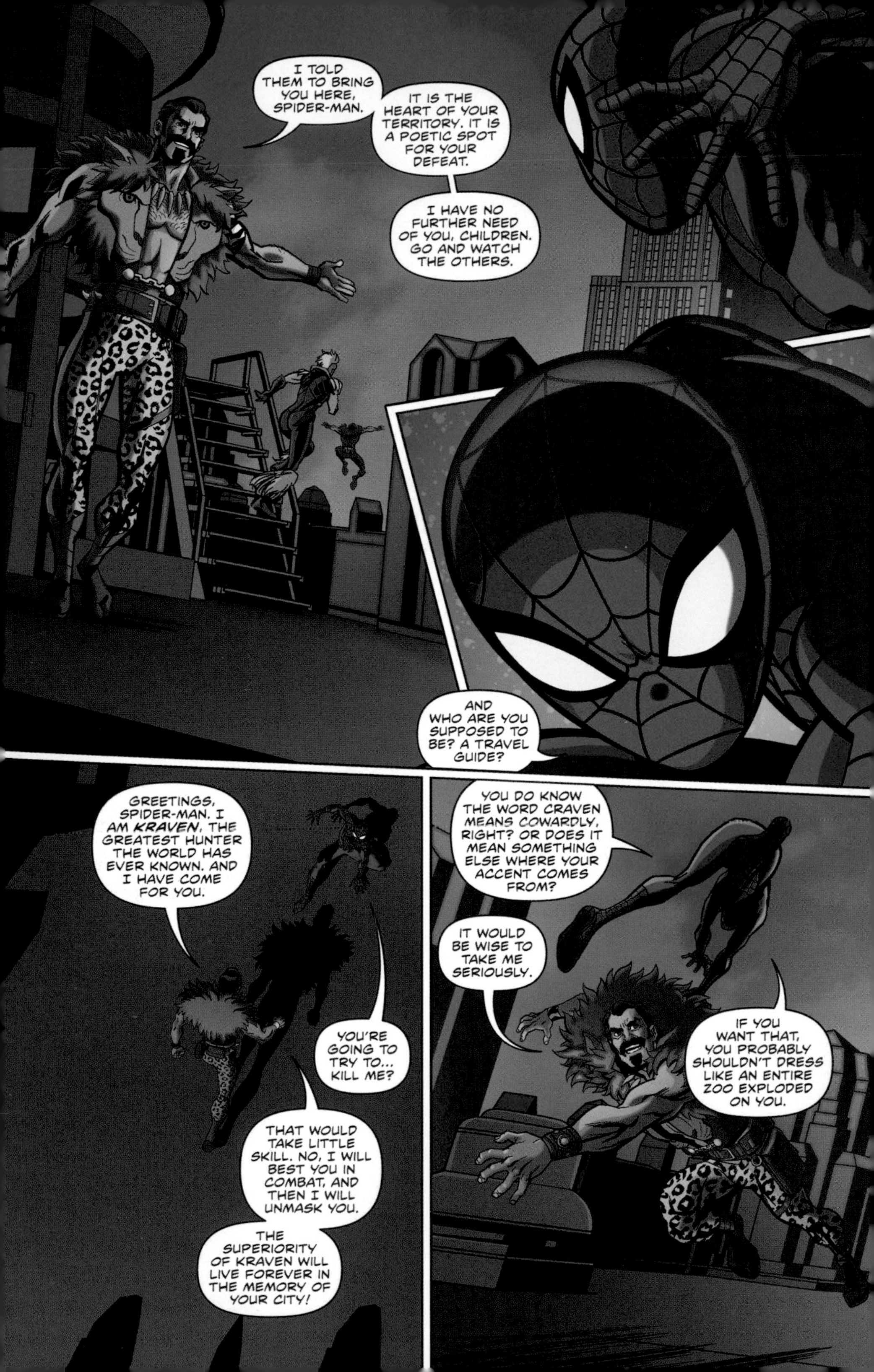

I TOLD THEM TO BRING YOU HERE, SPIDER-MAN.
IT IS THE HEART OF YOUR TERRITORY. IT IS A POETIC SPOT FOR YOUR DEFEAT.
I HAVE NO FURTHER NEED OF YOU, CHILDREN. GO AND WATCH THE OTHERS.
AND WHO ARE YOU SUPPOSED TO BE? A TRAVEL GUIDE?
GREETINGS, SPIDER-MAN. I AM *KRAVEN*, THE GREATEST HUNTER THE WORLD HAS EVER KNOWN. AND I HAVE COME FOR YOU.
YOU'RE GOING TO TRY TO... KILL ME?
THAT WOULD TAKE LITTLE SKILL. NO, I WILL BEST YOU IN COMBAT, AND THEN I WILL UNMASK YOU.
THE SUPERIORITY OF KRAVEN WILL LIVE FOREVER IN THE MEMORY OF YOUR CITY!
YOU DO KNOW THE WORD CRAVEN MEANS COWARDLY, RIGHT? OR DOES IT MEAN SOMETHING ELSE WHERE YOUR ACCENT COMES FROM?
IT WOULD BE WISE TO TAKE ME SERIOUSLY.
IF YOU WANT THAT, YOU PROBABLY SHOULDN'T DRESS LIKE AN ENTIRE ZOO EXPLODED ON YOU.

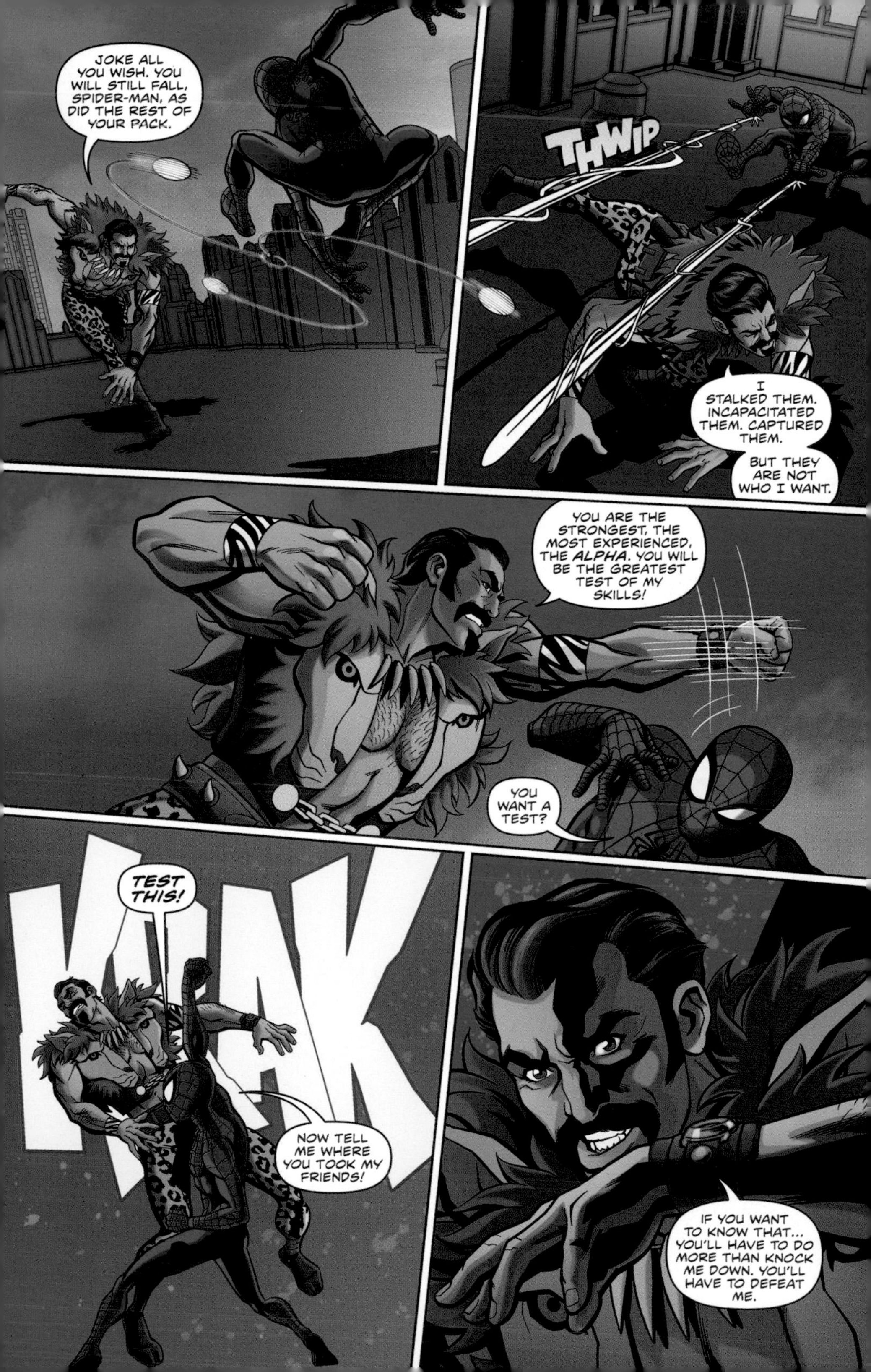
JOKE ALL YOU WISH. YOU WILL STILL FALL, SPIDER-MAN, AS DID THE REST OF YOUR PACK.
THWIP
I STALKED THEM. INCAPACITATED THEM. CAPTURED THEM.
BUT THEY ARE NOT WHO I WANT.
YOU ARE THE STRONGEST, THE MOST EXPERIENCED, THE *ALPHA*. YOU WILL BE THE GREATEST TEST OF MY SKILLS!
YOU WANT A TEST?
TEST THIS!
NOW TELL ME WHERE YOU TOOK MY FRIENDS!
IF YOU WANT TO KNOW THAT... YOU'LL HAVE TO DO MORE THAN KNOCK ME DOWN. YOU'LL HAVE TO DEFEAT ME.

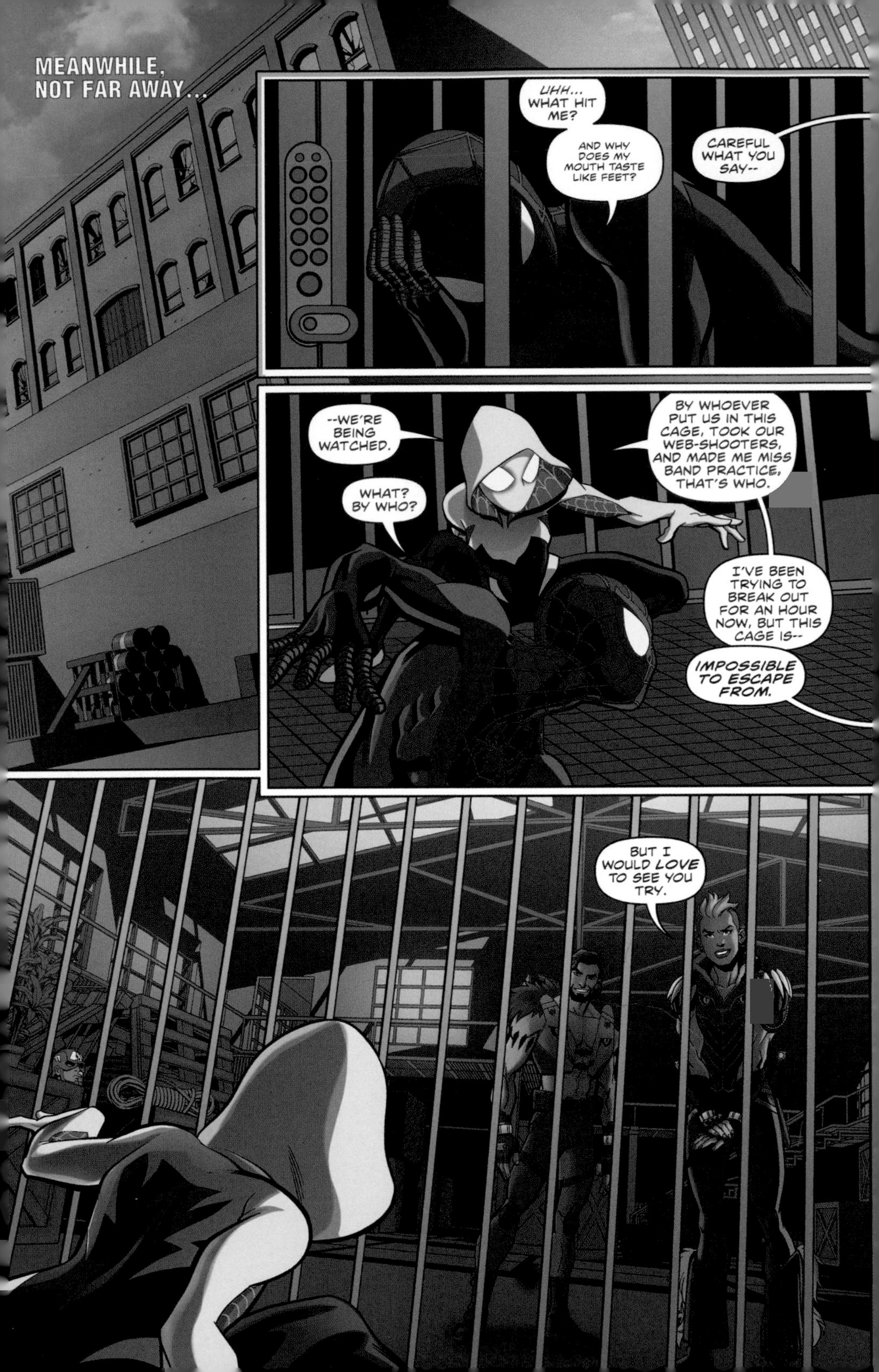
MEANWHILE, NOT FAR AWAY...
UHH... WHAT HIT ME?
AND WHY DOES MY MOUTH TASTE LIKE FEET?
CAREFUL WHAT YOU SAY--
--WE'RE BEING WATCHED.
WHAT? BY WHO?
BY WHOEVER PUT US IN THIS CAGE, TOOK OUR WEB-SHOOTERS, AND MADE ME MISS BAND PRACTICE, THAT'S WHO.
I'VE BEEN TRYING TO BREAK OUT FOR AN HOUR NOW, BUT THIS CAGE IS--
IMPOSSIBLE TO ESCAPE FROM.
BUT I WOULD LOVE TO SEE YOU TRY.

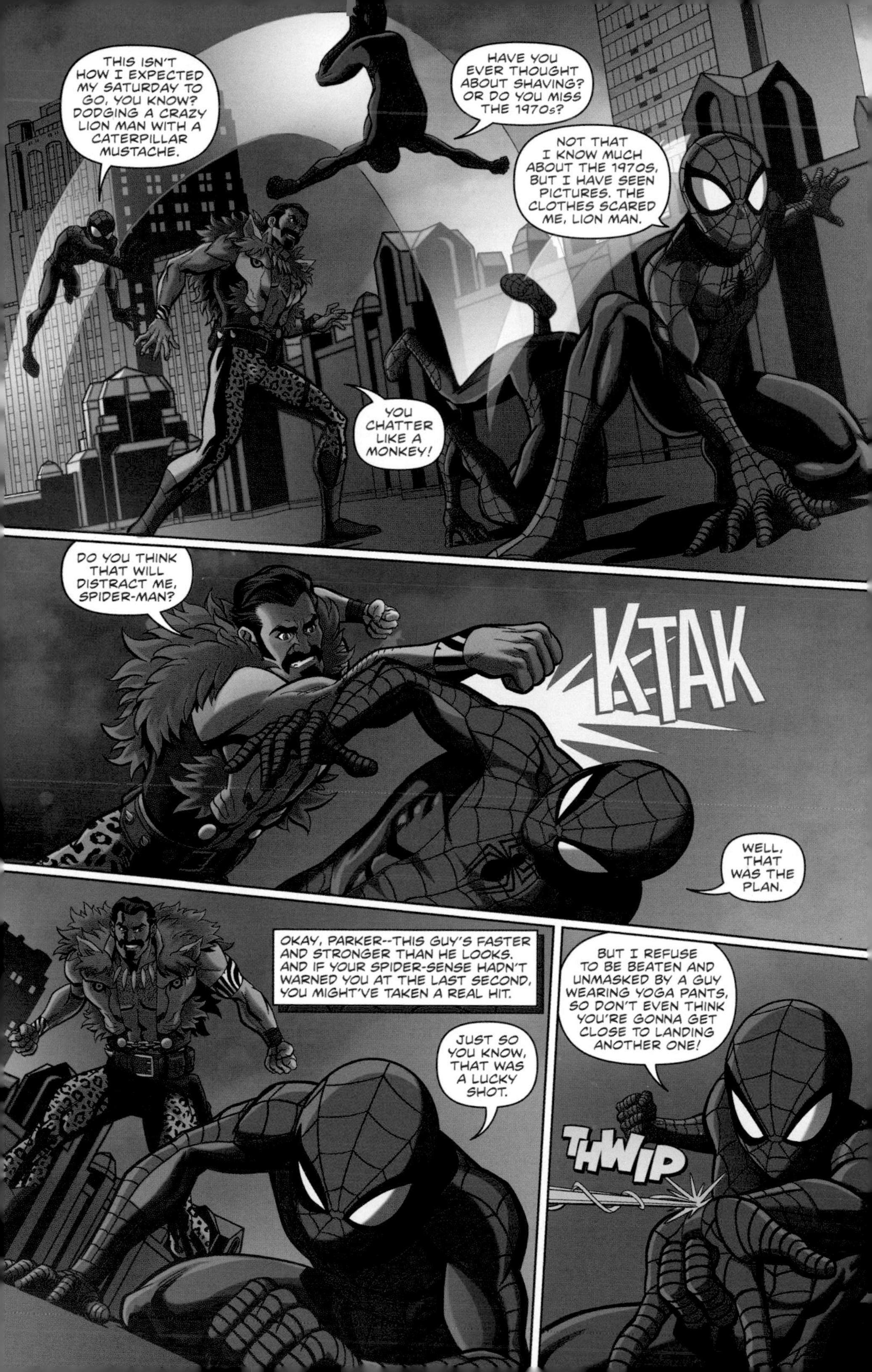
THIS ISN'T HOW I EXPECTED MY SATURDAY TO GO, YOU KNOW? DODGING A CRAZY LION MAN WITH A CATERPILLAR MUSTACHE.
HAVE YOU EVER THOUGHT ABOUT SHAVING? OR DO YOU MISS THE 1970s?
NOT THAT I KNOW MUCH ABOUT THE 1970S, BUT I HAVE SEEN PICTURES. THE CLOTHES SCARED ME, LION MAN.
YOU CHATTER LIKE A MONKEY!
DO YOU THINK THAT WILL DISTRACT ME, SPIDER-MAN?
K-TAK
WELL, THAT WAS THE PLAN.
OKAY, PARKER--THIS GUY'S FASTER AND STRONGER THAN HE LOOKS. AND IF YOUR SPIDER-SENSE HADN'T WARNED YOU AT THE LAST SECOND, YOU MIGHT'VE TAKEN A REAL HIT.
JUST SO YOU KNOW, THAT WAS A LUCKY SHOT.
BUT I REFUSE TO BE BEATEN AND UNMASKED BY A GUY WEARING YOGA PANTS, SO DON'T EVEN THINK YOU'RE GONNA GET CLOSE TO LANDING ANOTHER ONE!
THWIP

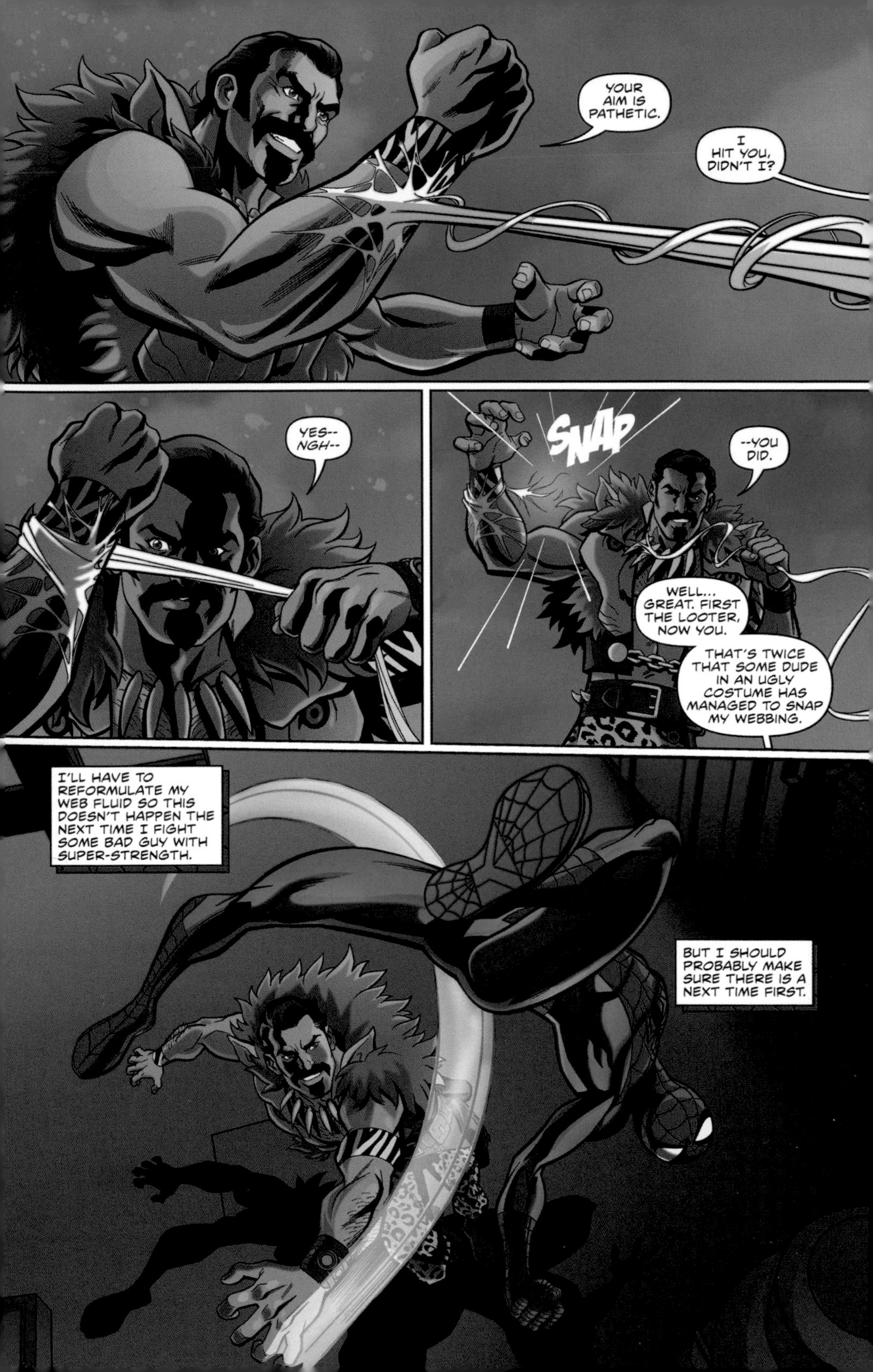

YOUR AIM IS PATHETIC.
I HIT YOU, DIDN'T I?
YES-- NGH--
SNAP
--YOU DID.
WELL... GREAT. FIRST THE LOOTER, NOW YOU.
THAT'S TWICE THAT SOME DUDE IN AN UGLY COSTUME HAS MANAGED TO SNAP MY WEBBING.
I'LL HAVE TO REFORMULATE MY WEB FLUID SO THIS DOESN'T HAPPEN THE NEXT TIME I FIGHT SOME BAD GUY WITH SUPER-STRENGTH.
BUT I SHOULD PROBABLY MAKE SURE THERE IS A NEXT TIME FIRST.

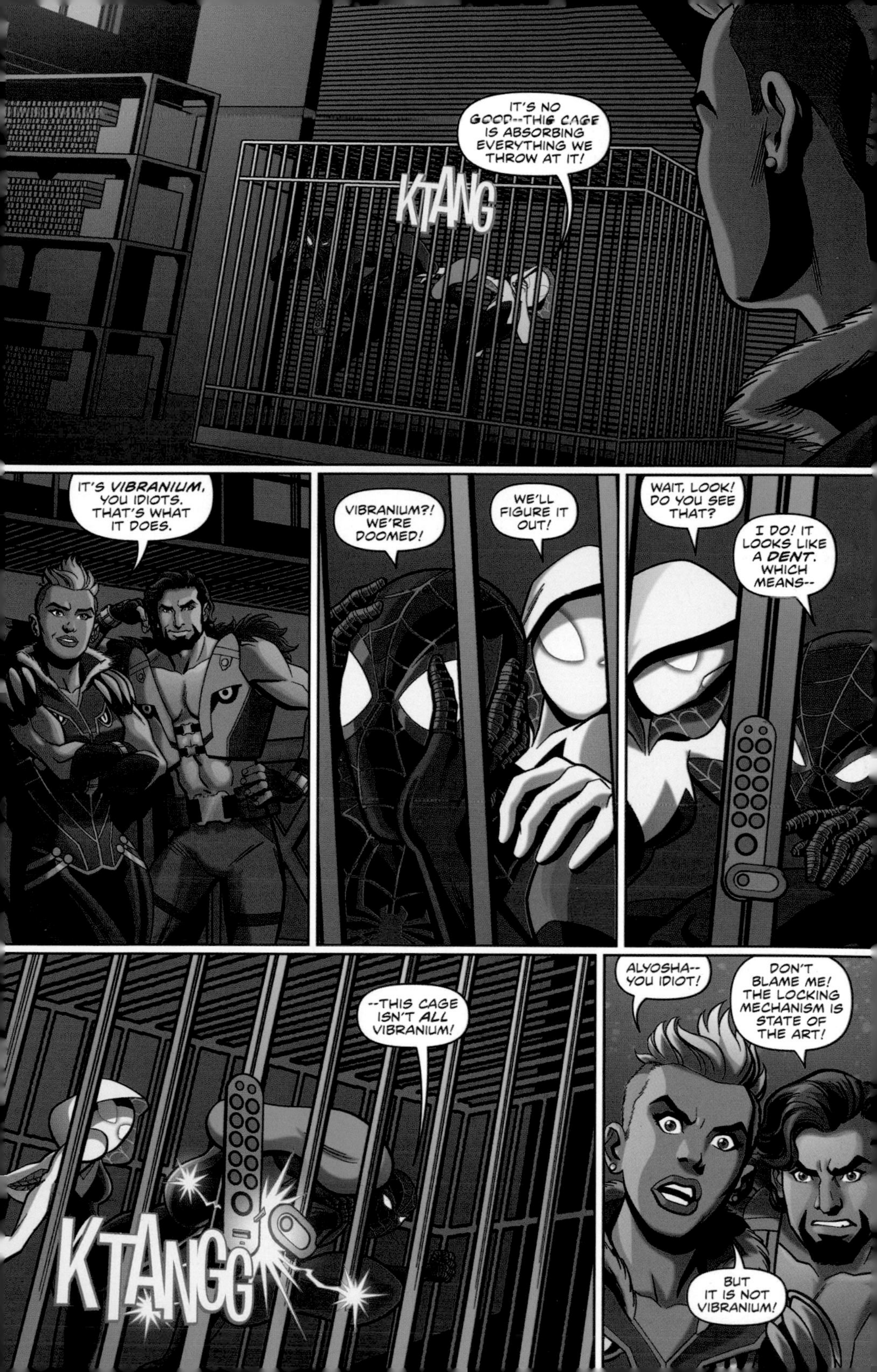

IT'S NO GOOD--THIS CAGE IS ABSORBING EVERYTHING WE THROW AT IT!
KTANG
IT'S VIBRANIUM, YOU IDIOTS. THAT'S WHAT IT DOES.
VIBRANIUM?! WE'RE DOOMED!
WE'LL FIGURE IT OUT!
WAIT, LOOK! DO YOU SEE THAT?
I DO! IT LOOKS LIKE A DENT. WHICH MEANS--
--THIS CAGE ISN'T ALL VIBRANIUM!
KTANGG
ALYOSHA-- YOU IDIOT!
DON'T BLAME ME! THE LOCKING MECHANISM IS STATE OF THE ART!
BUT IT IS NOT VIBRANIUM!

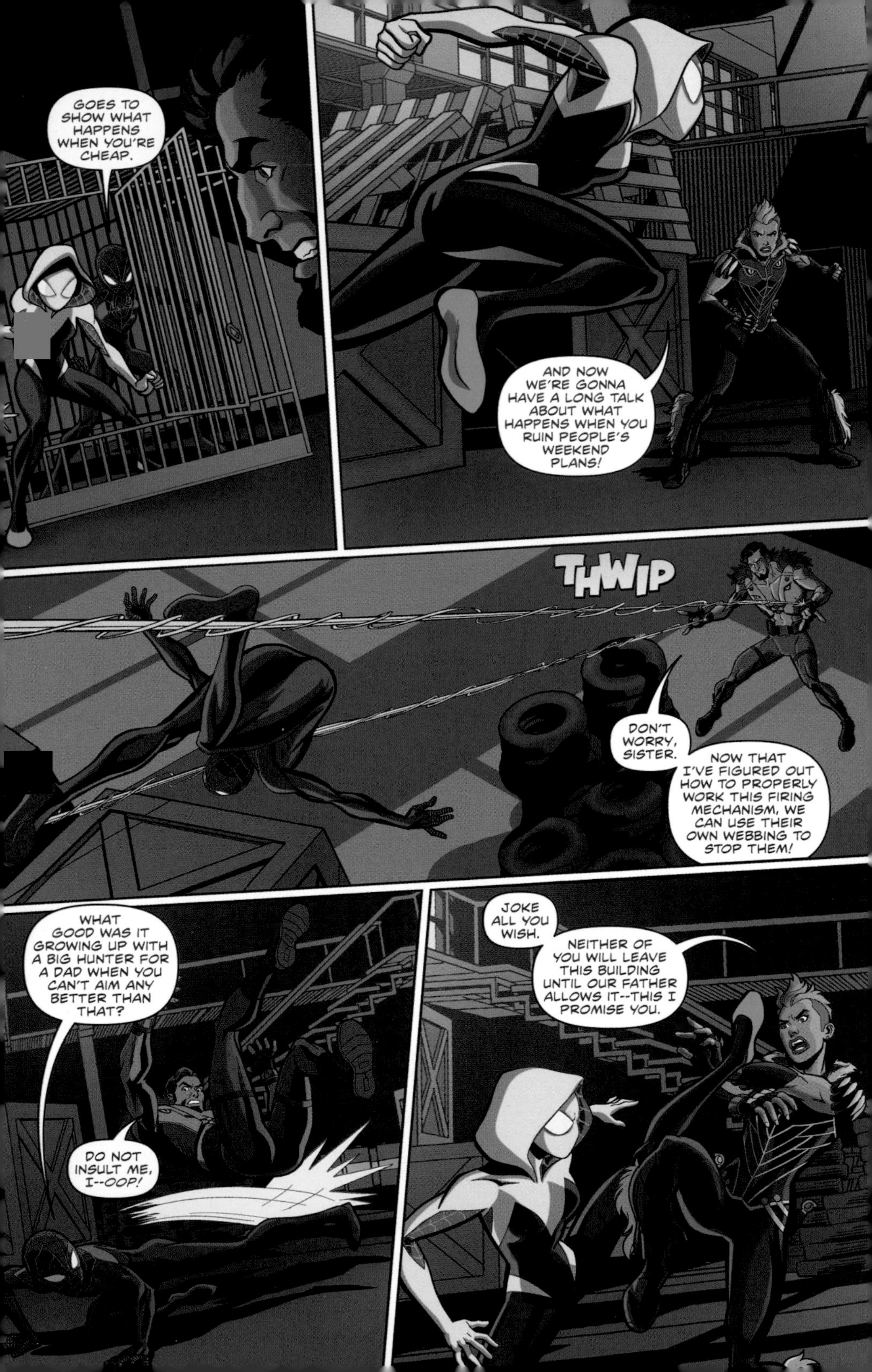
GOES TO SHOW WHAT HAPPENS WHEN YOU'RE CHEAP.
AND NOW WE'RE GONNA HAVE A LONG TALK ABOUT WHAT HAPPENS WHEN YOU RUIN PEOPLE'S WEEKEND PLANS!
THWIP
DON'T WORRY, SISTER.
NOW THAT I'VE FIGURED OUT HOW TO PROPERLY WORK THIS FIRING MECHANISM, WE CAN USE THEIR OWN WEBBING TO STOP THEM!
WHAT GOOD WAS IT GROWING UP WITH A BIG HUNTER FOR A DAD WHEN YOU CAN'T AIM ANY BETTER THAN THAT?
DO NOT INSULT ME, I--OOP!
JOKE ALL YOU WISH.
NEITHER OF YOU WILL LEAVE THIS BUILDING UNTIL OUR FATHER ALLOWS IT--THIS I PROMISE YOU.

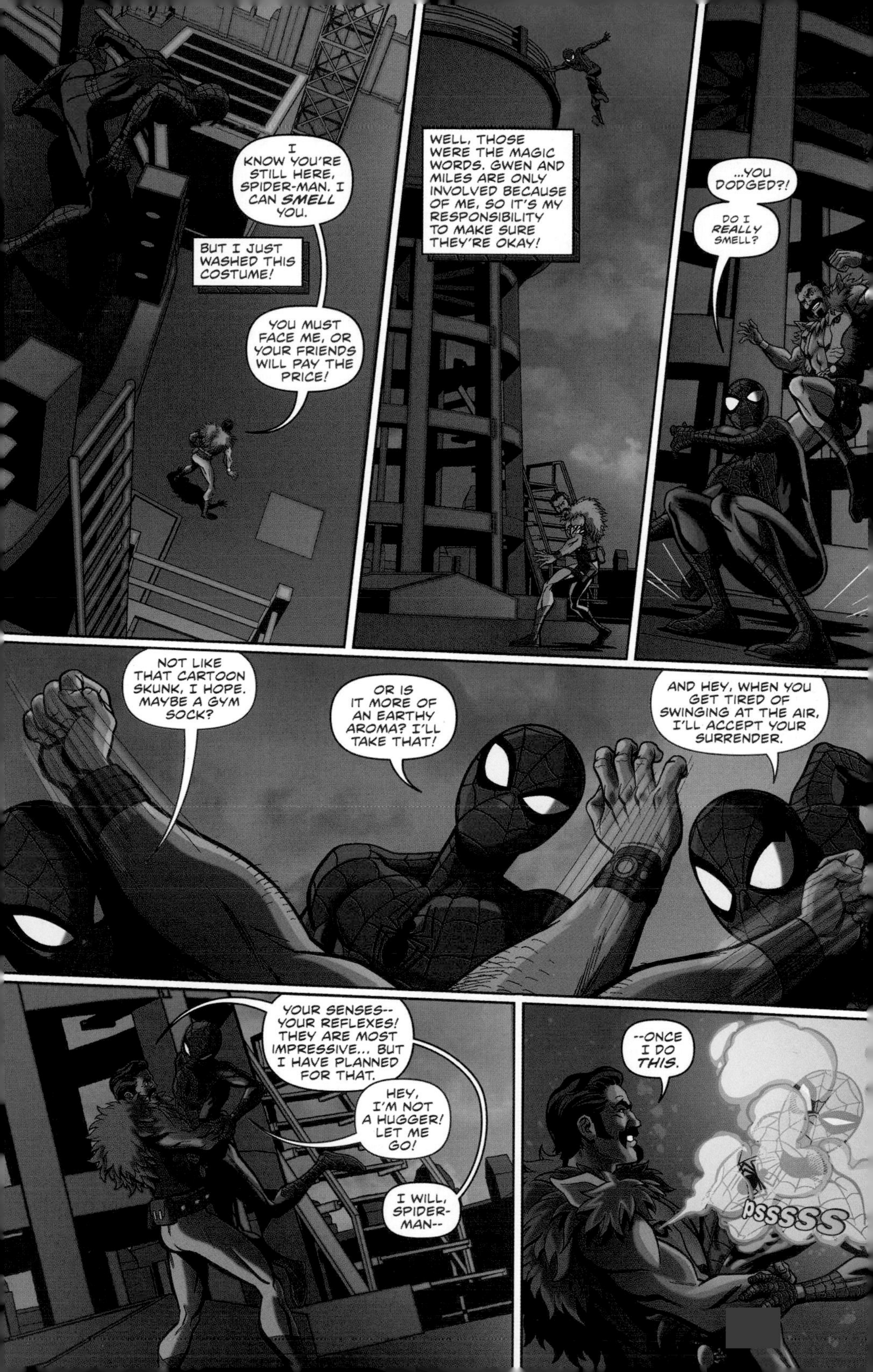
I KNOW YOU'RE STILL HERE, SPIDER-MAN. I CAN SMELL YOU.
BUT I JUST WASHED THIS COSTUME!
YOU MUST FACE ME, OR YOUR FRIENDS WILL PAY THE PRICE!
WELL, THOSE WERE THE MAGIC WORDS. GWEN AND MILES ARE ONLY INVOLVED BECAUSE OF ME, SO IT'S MY RESPONSIBILITY TO MAKE SURE THEY'RE OKAY!
...YOU DODGED?!
DO I REALLY SMELL?
NOT LIKE THAT CARTOON SKUNK, I HOPE. MAYBE A GYM SOCK?
OR IS IT MORE OF AN EARTHY AROMA? I'LL TAKE THAT!
AND HEY, WHEN YOU GET TIRED OF SWINGING AT THE AIR, I'LL ACCEPT YOUR SURRENDER.
YOUR SENSES-- YOUR REFLEXES! THEY ARE MOST IMPRESSIVE... BUT I HAVE PLANNED FOR THAT.
HEY, I'M NOT A HUGGER! LET ME GO!
I WILL, SPIDER-MAN--
--ONCE I DO THIS.
PSSSSS

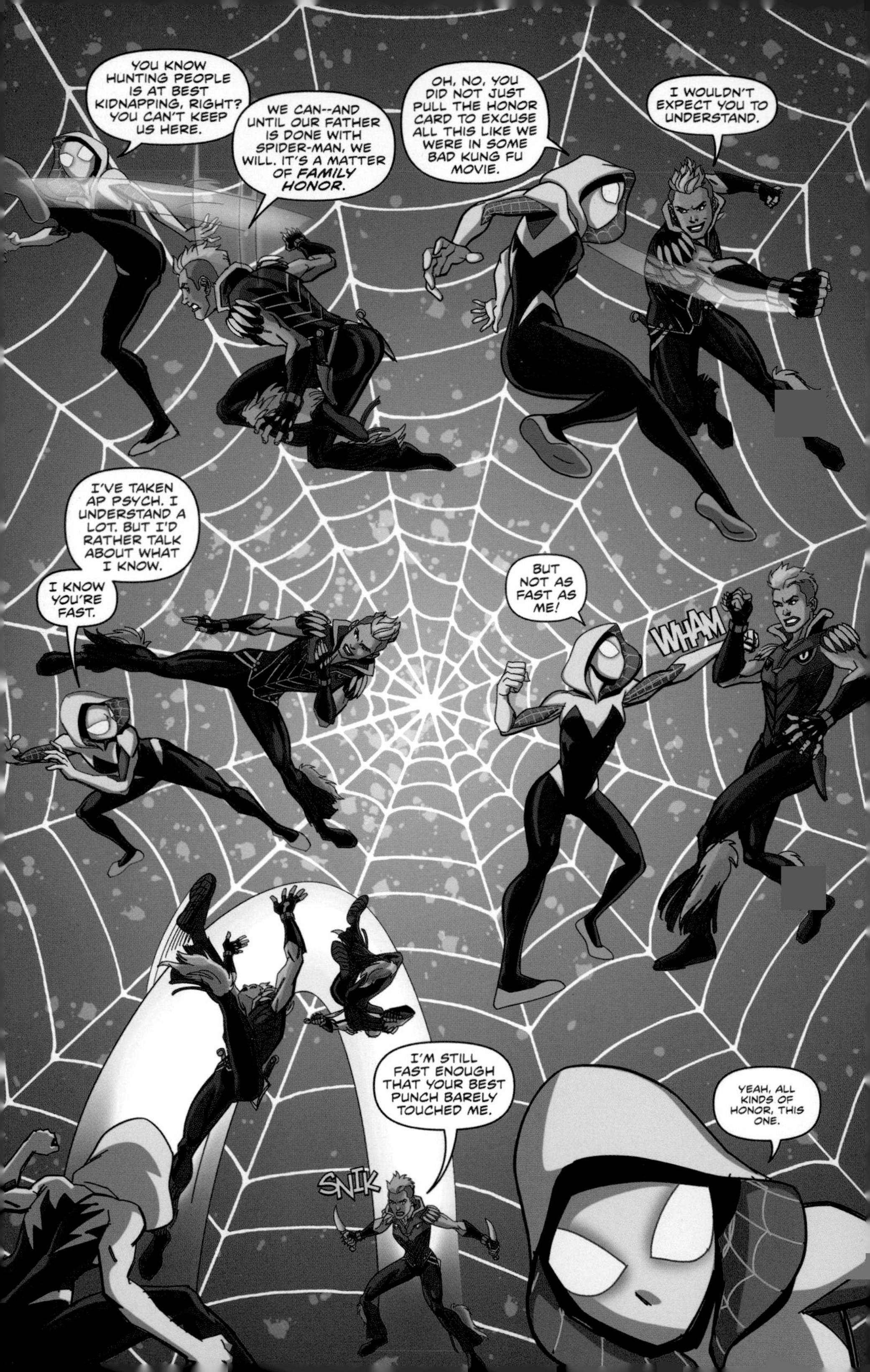
YOU KNOW HUNTING PEOPLE IS AT BEST KIDNAPPING, RIGHT? YOU CAN'T KEEP US HERE.
WE CAN--AND UNTIL OUR FATHER IS DONE WITH SPIDER-MAN, WE WILL. IT'S A MATTER OF FAMILY HONOR.
OH, NO, YOU DID NOT JUST PULL THE HONOR CARD TO EXCUSE ALL THIS LIKE WE WERE IN SOME BAD KUNG FU MOVIE.
I WOULDN'T EXPECT YOU TO UNDERSTAND.
I'VE TAKEN AP PSYCH. I UNDERSTAND A LOT. BUT I'D RATHER TALK ABOUT WHAT I KNOW.
I KNOW YOU'RE FAST.
BUT NOT AS FAST AS ME!
WHAM
I'M STILL FAST ENOUGH THAT YOUR BEST PUNCH BARELY TOUCHED ME.
SNIK
YEAH, ALL KINDS OF HONOR, THIS ONE.

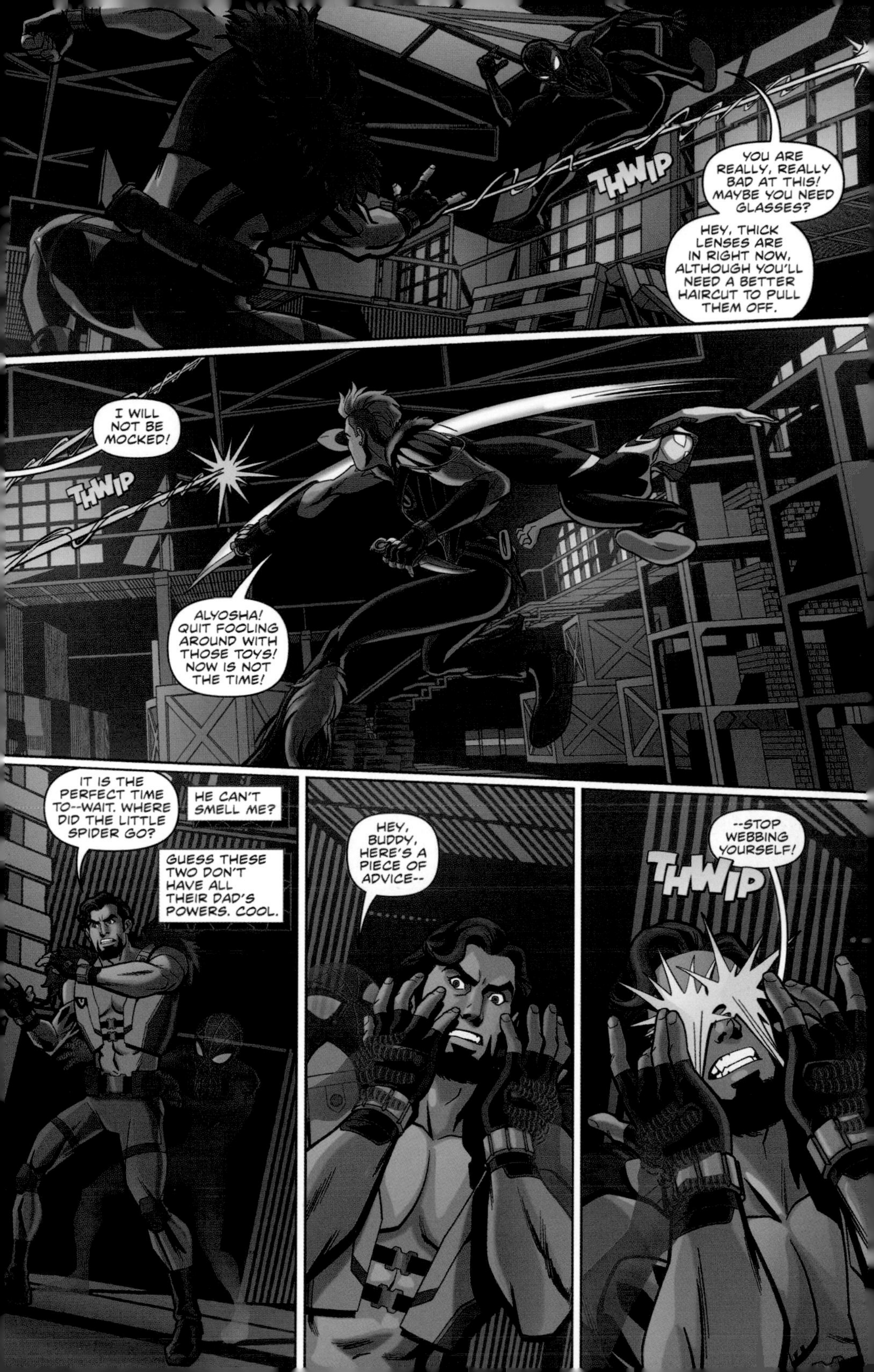
THWIP
YOU ARE REALLY, REALLY BAD AT THIS! MAYBE YOU NEED GLASSES?
HEY, THICK LENSES ARE IN RIGHT NOW, ALTHOUGH YOU'LL NEED A BETTER HAIRCUT TO PULL THEM OFF.
I WILL NOT BE MOCKED!
THWIP
ALYOSHA! QUIT FOOLING AROUND WITH THOSE TOYS! NOW IS NOT THE TIME!
IT IS THE PERFECT TIME TO--WAIT. WHERE DID THE LITTLE SPIDER GO?
HE CAN'T SMELL ME?
GUESS THESE TWO DON'T HAVE ALL THEIR DAD'S POWERS. COOL.
HEY, BUDDY, HERE'S A PIECE OF ADVICE--
THWIP
--STOP WEBBING YOURSELF!

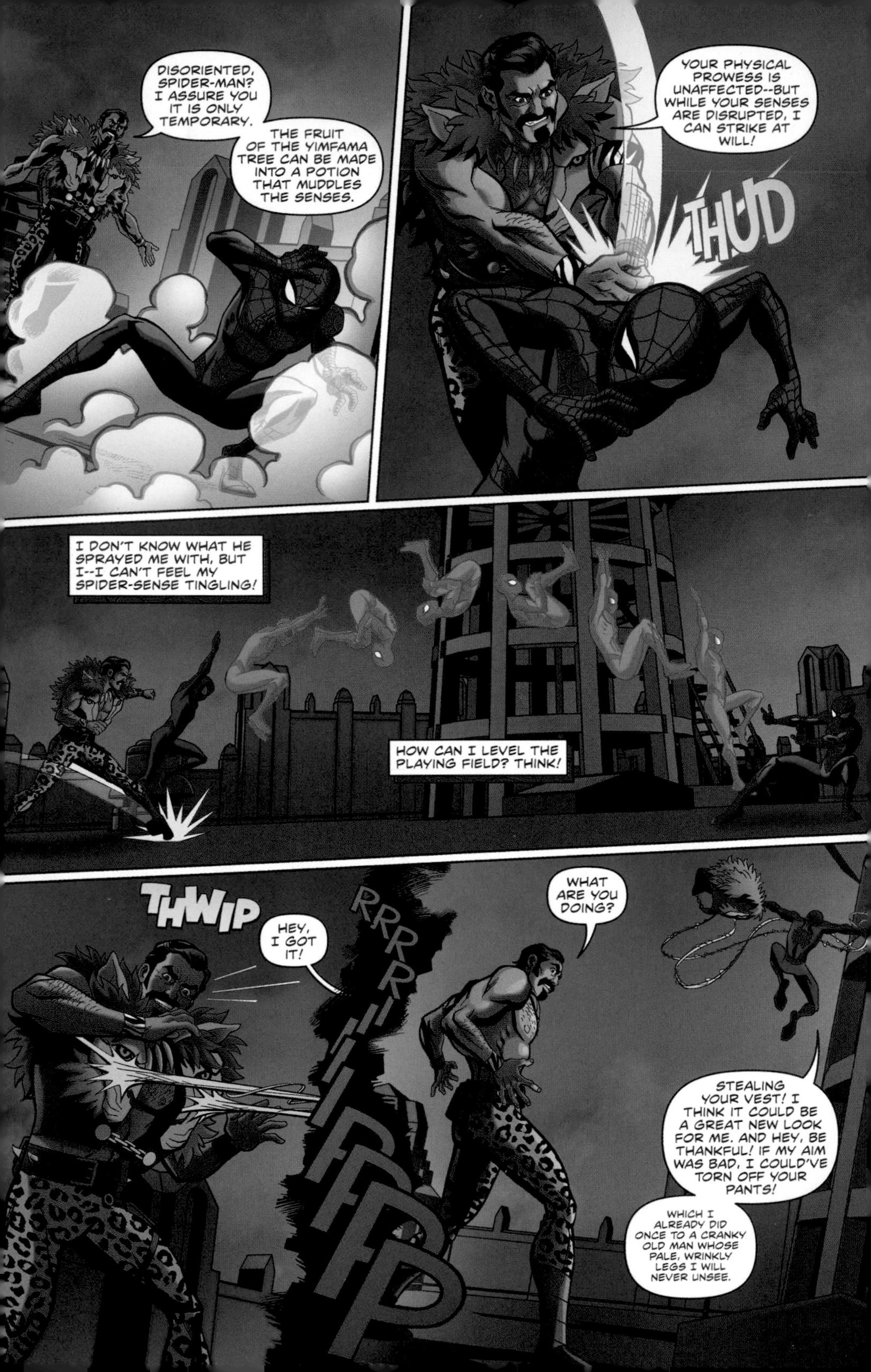
DISORIENTED, SPIDER-MAN? I ASSURE YOU IT IS ONLY TEMPORARY.
THE FRUIT OF THE YIMFAMA TREE CAN BE MADE INTO A POTION THAT MUDDLES THE SENSES.
YOUR PHYSICAL PROWESS IS UNAFFECTED--BUT WHILE YOUR SENSES ARE DISRUPTED, I CAN STRIKE AT WILL!
THUD
I DON'T KNOW WHAT HE SPRAYED ME WITH, BUT I--I CAN'T FEEL MY SPIDER-SENSE TINGLING!
HOW CAN I LEVEL THE PLAYING FIELD? THINK!
THWIP
HEY, I GOT IT!
RRRRIIIIPPPP
WHAT ARE YOU DOING?
STEALING YOUR VEST! I THINK IT COULD BE A GREAT NEW LOOK FOR ME. AND HEY, BE THANKFUL! IF MY AIM WAS BAD, I COULD'VE TORN OFF YOUR PANTS!
WHICH I ALREADY DID ONCE TO A CRANKY OLD MAN WHOSE PALE, WRINKLY LEGS I WILL NEVER UNSEE.

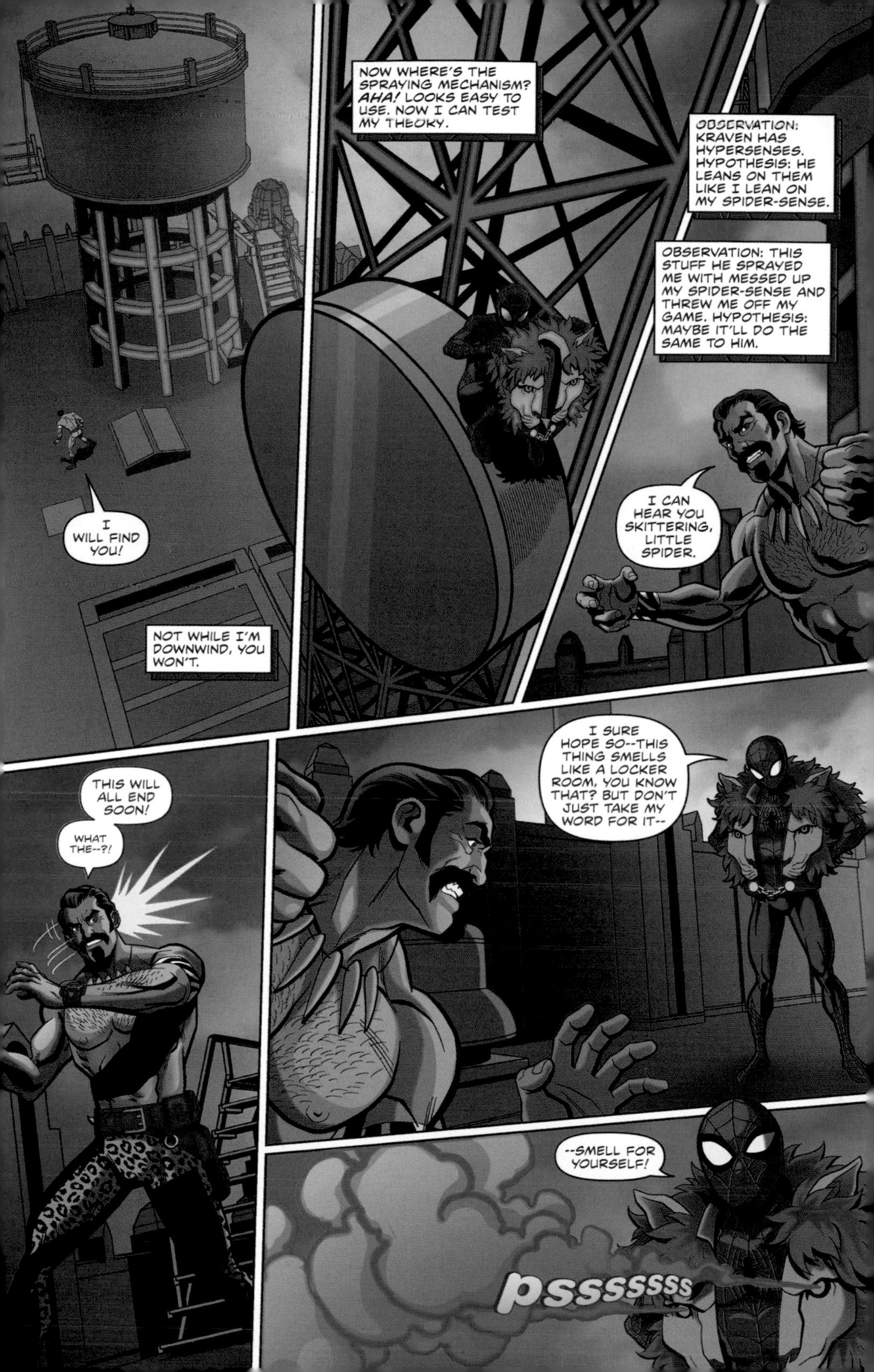
NOW WHERE'S THE SPRAYING MECHANISM? AHA! LOOKS EASY TO USE. NOW I CAN TEST MY THEORY.
I WILL FIND YOU!
NOT WHILE I'M DOWNWIND, YOU WON'T.
OBSERVATION: KRAVEN HAS HYPERSENSES. HYPOTHESIS: HE LEANS ON THEM LIKE I LEAN ON MY SPIDER-SENSE.
OBSERVATION: THIS STUFF HE SPRAYED ME WITH MESSED UP MY SPIDER-SENSE AND THREW ME OFF MY GAME. HYPOTHESIS: MAYBE IT'LL DO THE SAME TO HIM.
I CAN HEAR YOU SKITTERING, LITTLE SPIDER.
THIS WILL ALL END SOON!
WHAT THE--?!
I SURE HOPE SO--THIS THING SMELLS LIKE A LOCKER ROOM, YOU KNOW THAT? BUT DON'T JUST TAKE MY WORD FOR IT--
--SMELL FOR YOURSELF!
PSSSSSSS

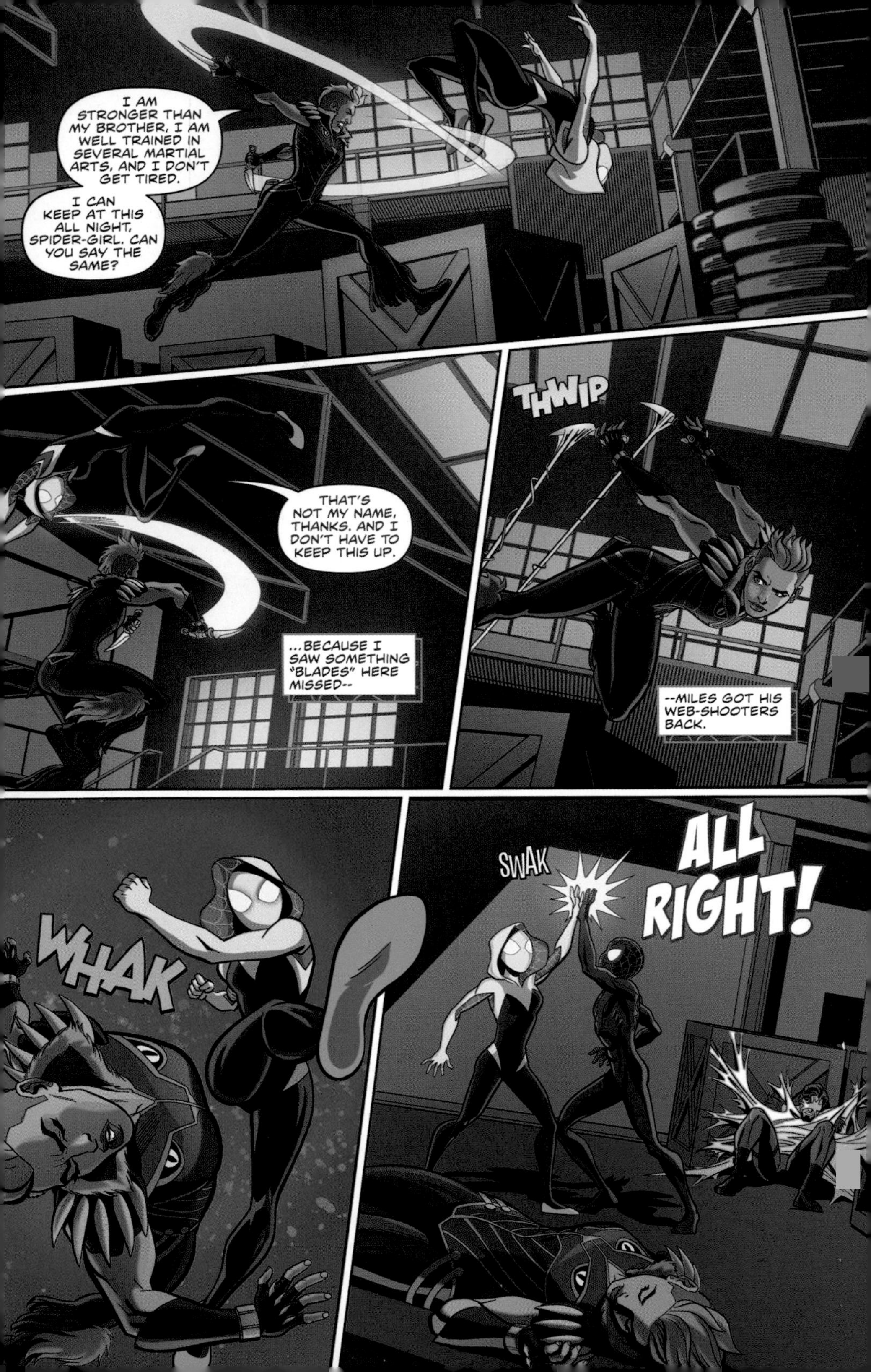
I AM STRONGER THAN MY BROTHER, I AM WELL TRAINED IN SEVERAL MARTIAL ARTS, AND I DON'T GET TIRED.
I CAN KEEP AT THIS ALL NIGHT, SPIDER-GIRL. CAN YOU SAY THE SAME?
THAT'S NOT MY NAME, THANKS. AND I DON'T HAVE TO KEEP THIS UP.
...BECAUSE I SAW SOMETHING "BLADES" HERE MISSED--
THWIP
--MILES GOT HIS WEB-SHOOTERS BACK.
WHAK
SWAK
ALL RIGHT!

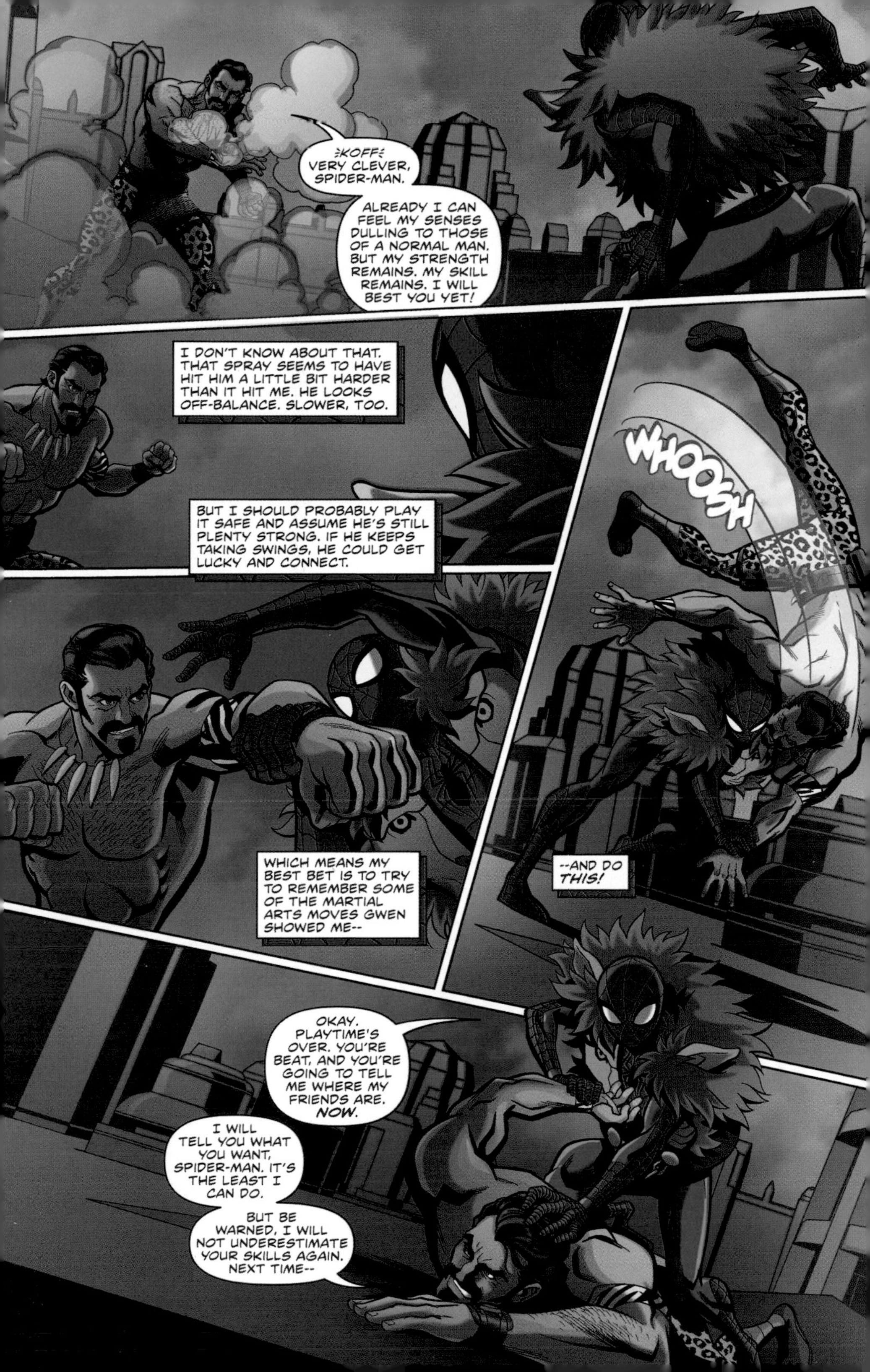

≡KOFF≡ VERY CLEVER, SPIDER-MAN.
ALREADY I CAN FEEL MY SENSES DULLING TO THOSE OF A NORMAL MAN. BUT MY STRENGTH REMAINS. MY SKILL REMAINS. I WILL BEST YOU YET!
I DON'T KNOW ABOUT THAT. THAT SPRAY SEEMS TO HAVE HIT HIM A LITTLE BIT HARDER THAN IT HIT ME. HE LOOKS OFF-BALANCE. SLOWER, TOO.
BUT I SHOULD PROBABLY PLAY IT SAFE AND ASSUME HE'S STILL PLENTY STRONG. IF HE KEEPS TAKING SWINGS, HE COULD GET LUCKY AND CONNECT.
WHICH MEANS MY BEST BET IS TO TRY TO REMEMBER SOME OF THE MARTIAL ARTS MOVES GWEN SHOWED ME--
WHOOSH
--AND DO *THIS!*
OKAY. PLAYTIME'S OVER. YOU'RE BEAT, AND YOU'RE GOING TO TELL ME WHERE MY FRIENDS ARE. **NOW**.
I WILL TELL YOU WHAT YOU WANT, SPIDER-MAN. IT'S THE LEAST I CAN DO.
BUT BE WARNED, I WILL NOT UNDERESTIMATE YOUR SKILLS AGAIN. NEXT TIME--

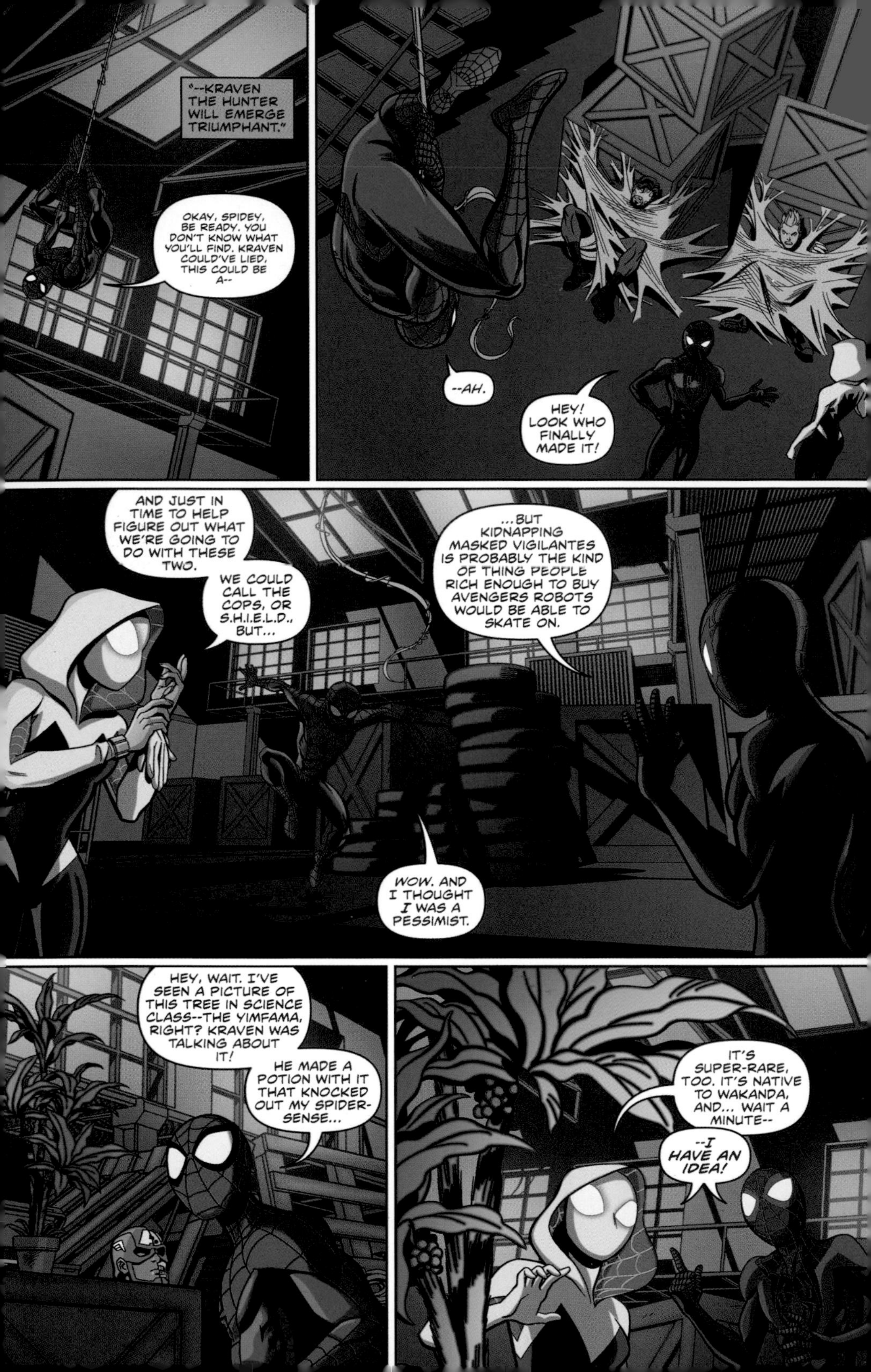
"--KRAVEN THE HUNTER WILL EMERGE TRIUMPHANT."
OKAY, SPIDEY, BE READY. YOU DON'T KNOW WHAT YOU'LL FIND. KRAVEN COULD'VE LIED, THIS COULD BE A--
--AH.
HEY! LOOK WHO FINALLY MADE IT!
AND JUST IN TIME TO HELP FIGURE OUT WHAT WE'RE GOING TO DO WITH THESE TWO.
WE COULD CALL THE COPS, OR S.H.I.E.L.D., BUT...
...BUT KIDNAPPING MASKED VIGILANTES IS PROBABLY THE KIND OF THING PEOPLE RICH ENOUGH TO BUY AVENGERS ROBOTS WOULD BE ABLE TO SKATE ON.
WOW. AND I THOUGHT I WAS A PESSIMIST.
HEY, WAIT. I'VE SEEN A PICTURE OF THIS TREE IN SCIENCE CLASS--THE YIMFAMA, RIGHT? KRAVEN WAS TALKING ABOUT IT!
HE MADE A POTION WITH IT THAT KNOCKED OUT MY SPIDER-SENSE...
IT'S SUPER-RARE, TOO. IT'S NATIVE TO WAKANDA, AND... WAIT A MINUTE--
--I HAVE AN IDEA!

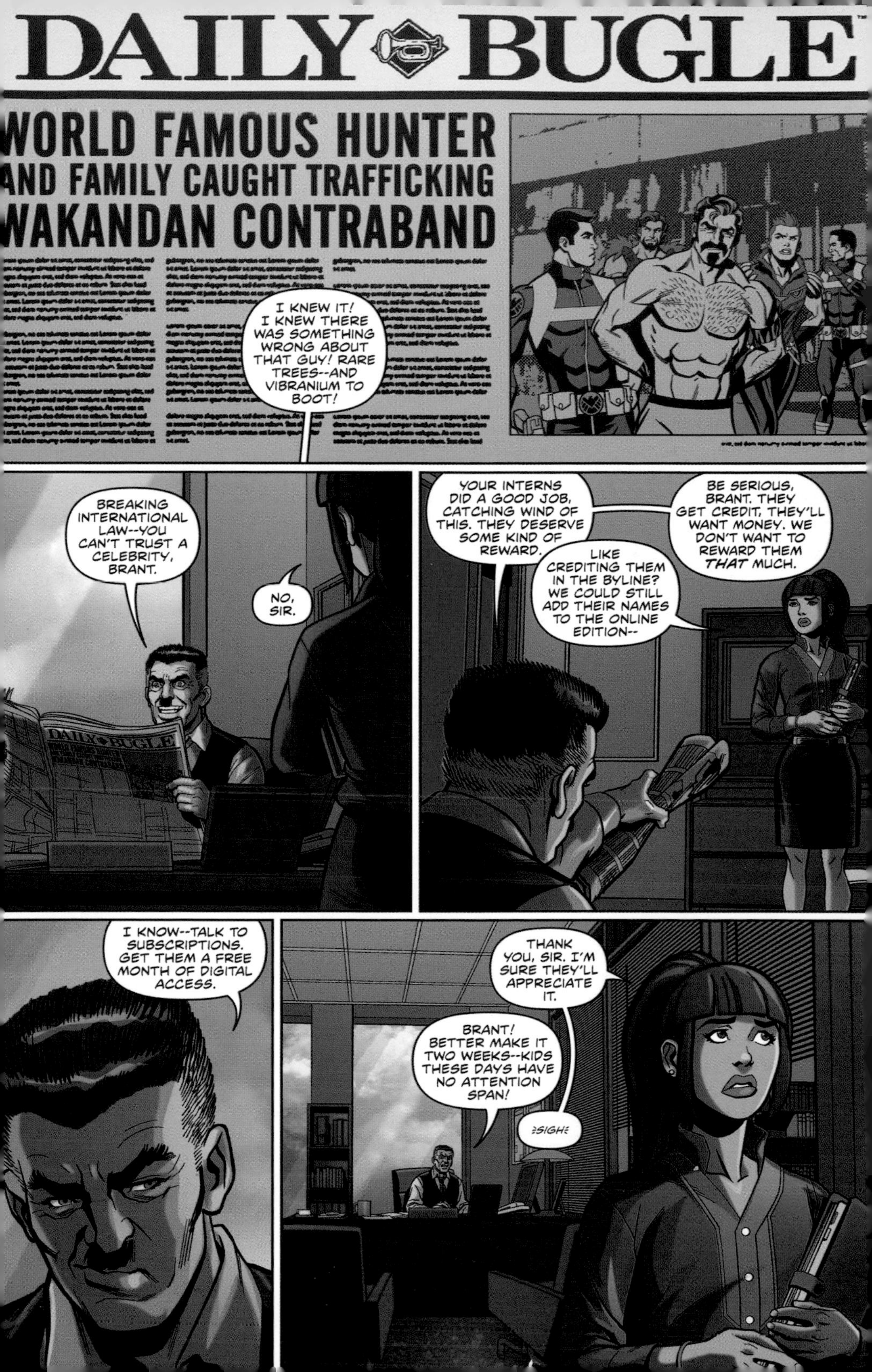
DAILY BUGLE
WORLD FAMOUS HUNTER AND FAMILY CAUGHT TRAFFICKING WAKANDAN CONTRABAND
I KNEW IT! I KNEW THERE WAS SOMETHING WRONG ABOUT THAT GUY! RARE TREES--AND VIBRANIUM TO BOOT!
BREAKING INTERNATIONAL LAW--YOU CAN'T TRUST A CELEBRITY, BRANT.
NO, SIR.
YOUR INTERNS DID A GOOD JOB, CATCHING WIND OF THIS. THEY DESERVE SOME KIND OF REWARD.
LIKE CREDITING THEM IN THE BYLINE? WE COULD STILL ADD THEIR NAMES TO THE ONLINE EDITION--
BE SERIOUS, BRANT. THEY GET CREDIT, THEY'LL WANT MONEY. WE DON'T WANT TO REWARD THEM *THAT* MUCH.
I KNOW--TALK TO SUBSCRIPTIONS. GET THEM A FREE MONTH OF DIGITAL ACCESS.
THANK YOU, SIR. I'M SURE THEY'LL APPRECIATE IT.
BRANT! BETTER MAKE IT TWO WEEKS--KIDS THESE DAYS HAVE NO ATTENTION SPAN!
SIGH

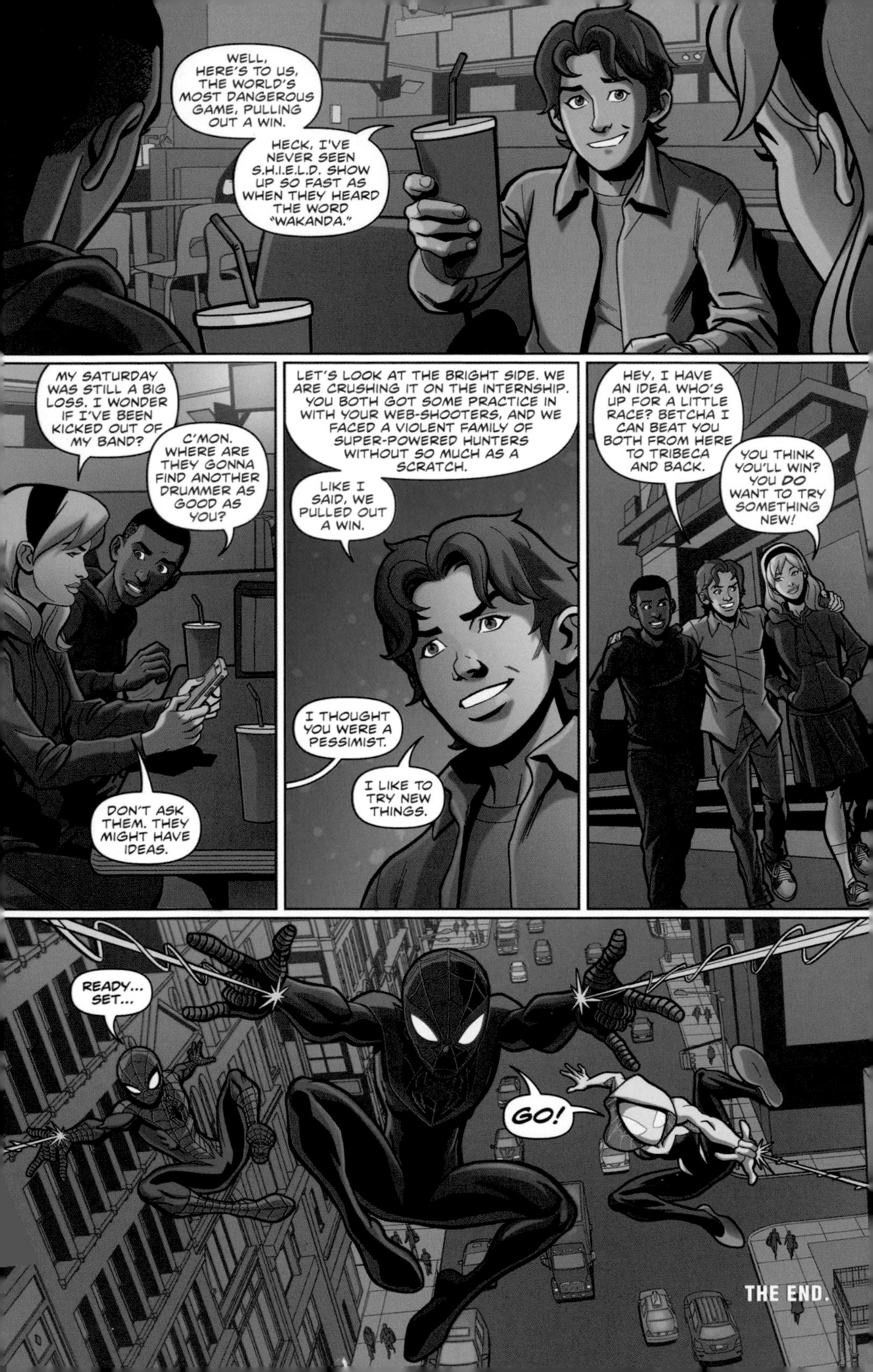
WELL, HERE'S TO US, THE WORLD'S MOST DANGEROUS GAME, PULLING OUT A WIN.
HECK, I'VE NEVER SEEN S.H.I.E.L.D. SHOW UP SO FAST AS WHEN THEY HEARD THE WORD "WAKANDA."
MY SATURDAY WAS STILL A BIG LOSS. I WONDER IF I'VE BEEN KICKED OUT OF MY BAND?
C'MON. WHERE ARE THEY GONNA FIND ANOTHER DRUMMER AS GOOD AS YOU?
DON'T ASK THEM. THEY MIGHT HAVE IDEAS.
LET'S LOOK AT THE BRIGHT SIDE. WE ARE CRUSHING IT ON THE INTERNSHIP. YOU BOTH GOT SOME PRACTICE IN WITH YOUR WEB-SHOOTERS, AND WE FACED A VIOLENT FAMILY OF SUPER-POWERED HUNTERS WITHOUT SO MUCH AS A SCRATCH.
LIKE I SAID, WE PULLED OUT A WIN.
I THOUGHT YOU WERE A PESSIMIST.
I LIKE TO TRY NEW THINGS.
HEY, I HAVE AN IDEA. WHO'S UP FOR A LITTLE RACE? BETCHA I CAN BEAT YOU BOTH FROM HERE TO TRIBECA AND BACK.
YOU THINK YOU'LL WIN? YOU DO WANT TO TRY SOMETHING NEW!
READY... SET...
GO!
THE END.

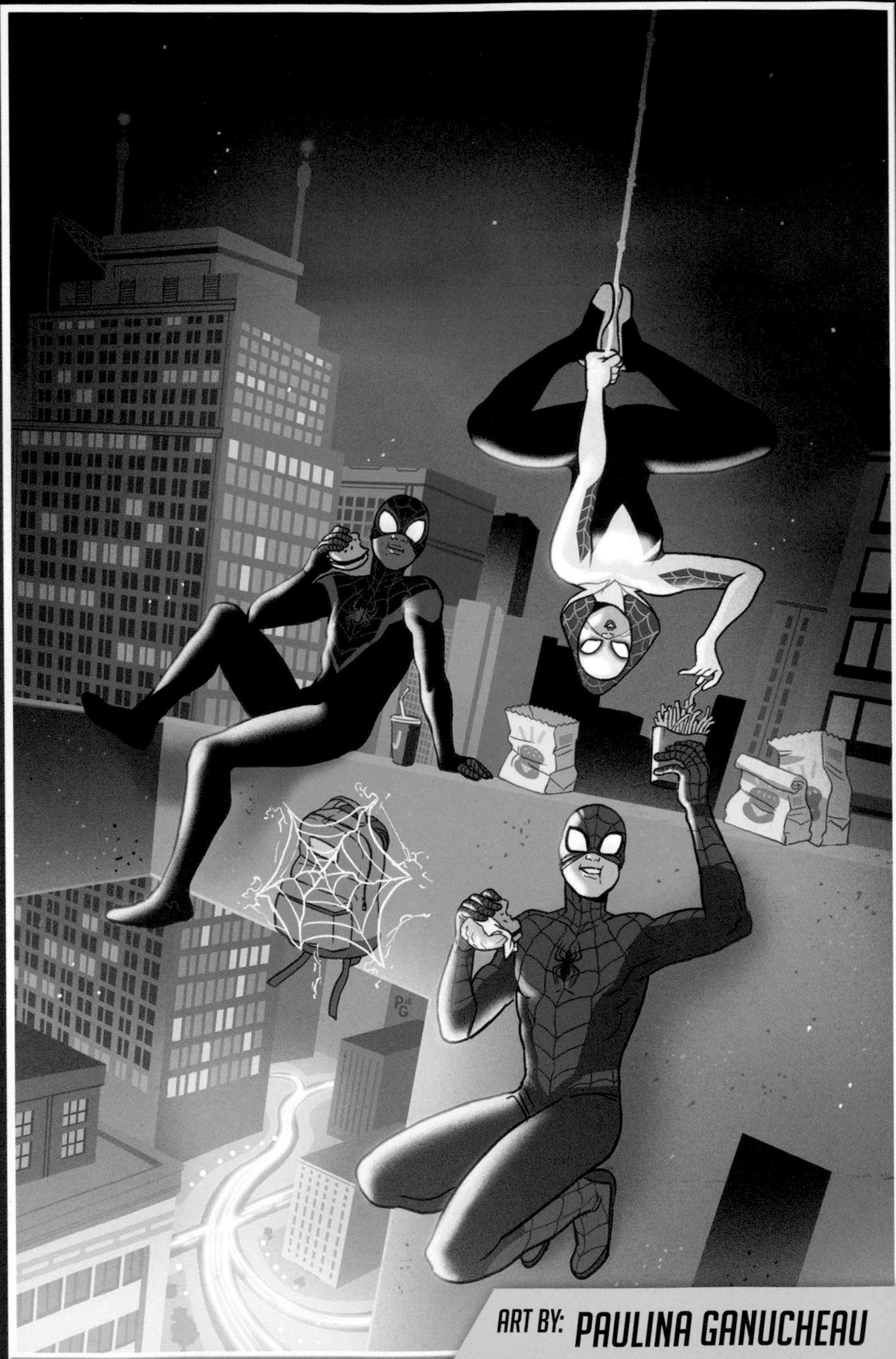
J
PG '18

ART BY: PAULINA GANUCHEAU

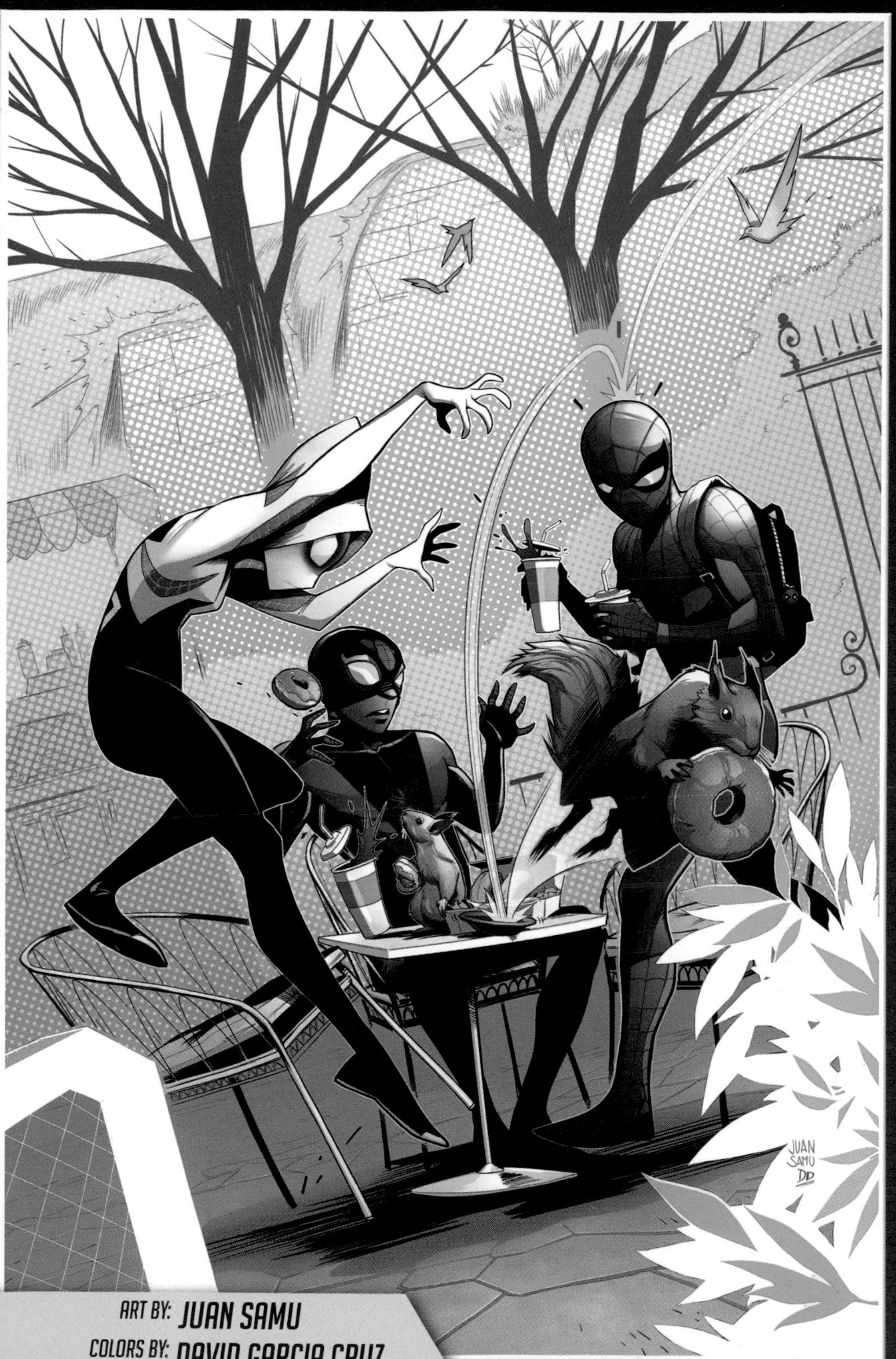
JUAN SAMU DD

ART BY: JUAN SAMU
COLORS BY: DAVID GARCIA CRUZ

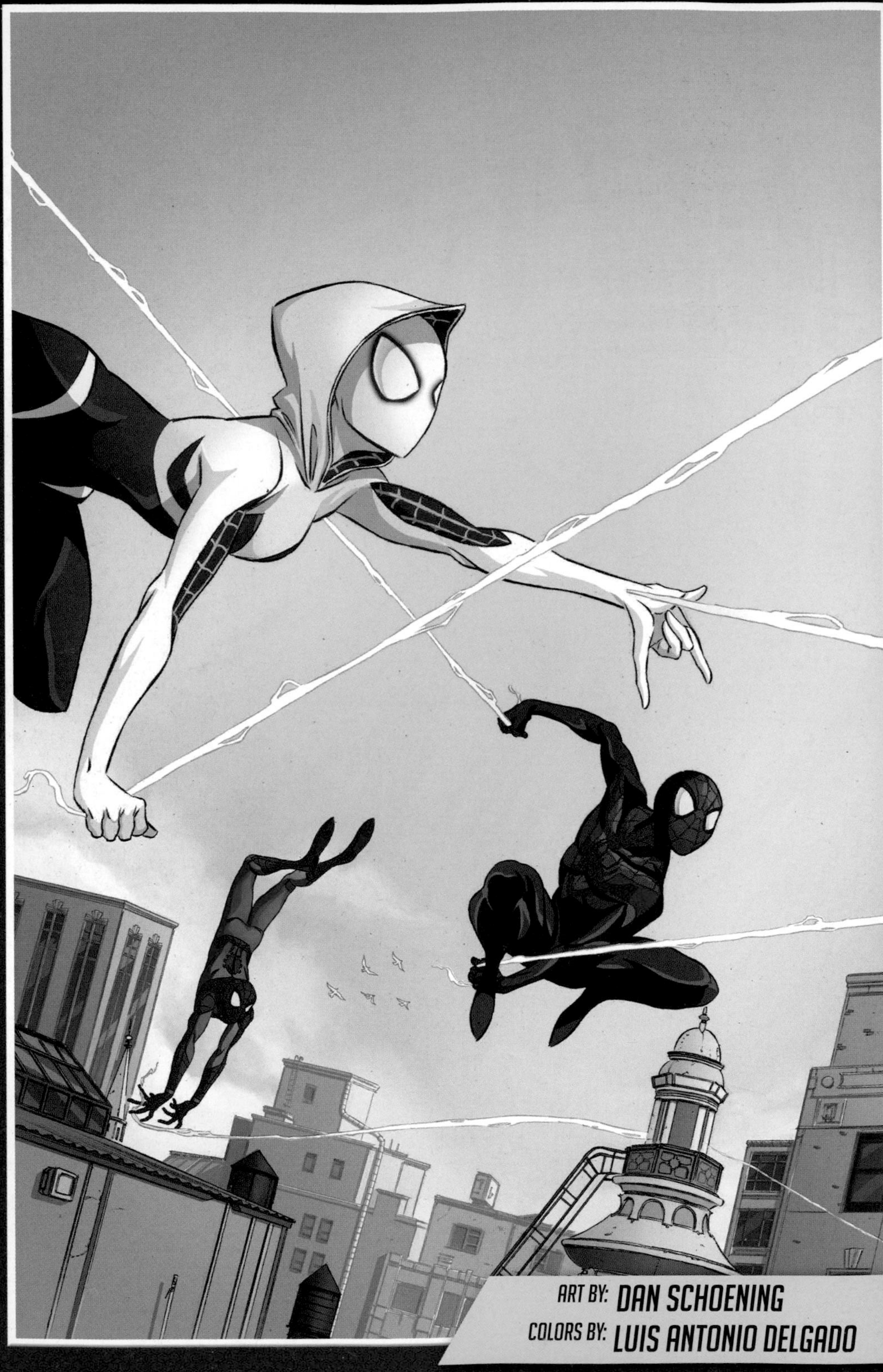
ART BY: DAN SCHOENING
COLORS BY: LUIS ANTONIO DELGADO